BOOK ONE OF
THE DARK MATTER SERIES

DEMON ZERO

Demon Zero is a work of fiction. The characters, incidents, and dialogue are drawn from the author's imagination and are not to be construed as real. Any resemblance to actual events or persons, living or dead, is entirely coincidental.

Copyright © 2018 by Clayton Smith

All rights reserved. Except as permitted under the U.S. Copyright Act of 1976, no part of this publication may be reproduced or used in any manner whatsoever without the express written permission of the publisher except for the use of brief quotations in a book review.

Printed in the United States of America

First Printing, 2018

ISBN 978-1-945747-04-5

Cover art and design by Steven Luna

*For A. G. Stevens, who was somehow
convinced that this would be a good idea.*

BOOK ONE OF
THE DARK MATTER SERIES

DEMON ZERO

CLAYTON SMITH

CHAPTER 1

"I'm not saying there's *not* a demon in Mrs. Grunberg's basement," Simon sighed. "I'm just saying that if there *is* a demon, we're not equipped to deal with it."

"Come on, Simon!" Virgil said, throwing up his hands in frustration. "If not us, who?"

"No one. *No one* is equipped to deal with demons. That's the thing about being a human person. You don't come naturally equipped with demon-hunting skills."

"Priests do," Virgil pointed out.

"Not all priests."

"Exorcists do. They're priests."

Simon ruffled his short blond hair and rubbed his hands down his face. The spinning, colored lights were really starting to hurt his eyes. "Why do we always come to Squeezy Cheez?" he complained.

"Because I work the morning shift at a ball bearing plant, and Squeezy Cheez is the only thing that brings me joy. Mostly, it's the Skee-Ball. Skee-Ball brings me joy."

"I hate Skee-Ball," Simon said miserably.

"And the pizza," Virgil pointed out, lifting another slice and chopping through the stringy cheese with one finger. "We come for that, too."

"The pizza is terrible," Simon pointed out.

"That's what makes it great."

Simon looked down sadly at the pizza. The sausage was weirdly pale, and clammy. He picked up a piece and jammed it into his mouth anyway. "Exorcists don't really apply here," he continued, mumbling through the cardboard crust. "They fight demons on a person's *inside*. Mrs. Grunberg's demon is on the *outside*."

"So you admit Mrs. Grunberg has a demon."

"I never said she didn't have a demon!" Simon said, exasperated. "It's just that if there *is* a demon in her basement, we're not...hey." He snapped his fingers. "Are you listening to me?"

Virgil's attention had wandered. "Is that a new Pop-A-Shot?" he asked, craning his neck to get a better view of the far side of the game room.

"Who cares about a Pop-A-Shot?"

"I do. I care about a Pop-A-Shot. I have long arms, I'm really good at Pop-A-Shot." He chewed thoughtfully on his bottom lip. "I could get a lot of tickets out of Pop-A-Shot."

"Look—"

"I need, like, three hundred more tickets, and the Nerf gun is mine. Also, did you see there's a new girl working the counter?" he asked, jerking his thumb toward the cash register. A woman about their age stood behind it, drumming her fingers on the counter, bored. She had pale skin, almost translucent, and her hair was dyed bright purple and cut into a cute bob. She had to stand on her tiptoes to reach even the bottom shelf of prizes, Simon had noticed.

"Yeah, I saw. So what?"

"So it's weird, isn't it? People in their twenties aren't supposed to work at Squeezy Cheez."

"I walk dogs for a living," Simon pointed out miserably.

"That's not *all* you do," Virgil said. Simon had a lot of odd jobs, and Virgil knew he was self-conscious about not having an actual career.

"Look, are we talking about demons or not?" Simon demanded.

"Yes, fine, let's talk about demons," Virgil said, turning back in his chair and rolling his eyes.

"You're the one who brought it up!" Simon cried.

"Well *someone* had to! It's going to eat poor Mrs. Grunberg!"

Simon pushed himself up from the table and pulled a wad of bills from his pocket. He tossed them down, then turned and walked out of restaurant.

"Hey!" Virgil cried. He jumped up from his seat, rifled through his wallet, and pulled out a ten. He threw it down on the table and ran after his roommate. He stopped about halfway to the door, hurried back to the table, and jammed another piece of pizza between his teeth. Then he sprinted across the restaurant, nearly knocking over a pair of twins on his way out the door. "Simon, come on! Stop!"

"I'm not doing this today," Simon said, fumbling for his keys and squinting in the sudden brightness of the sunlight. "I'm not getting sucked into your...your *vortex* of nonsense."

"You love my vortex of nonsense."

"Not today." Simon reached the old, beat-up Pontiac 6000LE that his grandmother had left him in her will. What paint was left was a dark maroon color, but most of that had flaked away, leaving a sickly silver metal showing through the rust. He jammed the key into the lock and grunted as he tried to turn it. "Stupid car," he muttered.

Virgil slipped on a trickle of oil on the asphalt and lost his balance, slamming into the side of the Pontiac. The muffler fell off with a clang.

"Oh, great," Simon grumbled.

"Sorry. Look." Virgil rubbed his elbow, which had slammed into the car window. "I'm sorry. It's just...don't you want to *do* something? Don't you want to *help* people?"

Simon sighed. He let go of the key, his lucky dice keychain dangling from the lock. "I don't *not* want to help people," he said. "But a demon? In Mrs. Grunberg's basement? Virgil, that's not our problem."

"I *know* it's not our problem. But that's exactly why it's our problem! Don't you get that?"

Simon blinked. "No," he answered honestly. "I don't."

"A demon in Mrs. Grunberg's basement isn't our problem. It's not *anyone's* problem. It's hardly even Mrs. Grunberg's problem, I doubt she could take manage a flight of stairs...she's 300 years old."

"She's 87."

"Her demon isn't anyone else's problem," Virgil continued. "The thing that crawled out of Gossamer Lake last month wasn't anyone's problem. That gross sewer monster that bubbled up on Ridge Road this year wasn't anyone's problem. Weird things happen in Templar, Simon. I don't know why Pennsylvania is some whirlpool of awful, but things happen here, dangerous things, *supernatural* things, and people go missing, or they go mad, or their bodies end up broken into pieces and scattered on the subway tracks, and it's never anyone's problem. That's why it has to be *someone's* problem. Let's *do* something!" he cried. "Let's *save* people! Let's go down to Mrs. Grunberg's basement and send her demon back to hell!"

Simon's face flushed red with anger. He pulled back against the instinct to slam his fist into the window of the Pontiac. But when his voice came out, it was small, and sad. "Do you even know what today is?" he whispered.

Virgil exhaled. He pinched the bridge of his nose between his fingers, and he shook his head. "Of course I know what today is," he replied. "How could I forget it? Of *course* I know."

Simon looked at his best friend, his eyes wet, his face pleading. "Then why are we talking about this today?"

The pain in his voice broke Virgil in half.

"We're talking about this today *because* it's today," Virgil said gently. He gave Simon a soft punch on the arm. "She's the reason we need to do this, Simon."

Simon lowered his eyes. He stared down at the car door, lost in his own thoughts, his eyes clouded over with memory. Finally, after several long moments, he spoke: "We couldn't have helped her."

Virgil dug into his palm with his thumb. "But we could help the next person," he said quietly.

Simon shot him a hard look. His eyes were rimmed red with the threat of tears. "We don't know the first thing about fighting demons, or sewer monsters, or lake serpents. Yeah, Virgil, weird things happen in Templar. Awful things. *Evil* things. I don't know why those things happen here, I don't know why the rest of the world looks at us and loses their minds and seals us off and leaves us for dead, I don't know why we live in the one city in the Western world with a direct line to an otherworldly hellstorm, but I *do* know why it *keeps* happening, with impunity: because there are no heroes in Templar. There are no more magics, or mages, or wizards, or gods, there is no one here to fight whatever it is that sends ghouls and vampires and banshees into our streets, and all we can do is pack our bags and leave this terrible, awful, evil city. There's no one here to save us, but it's too hard to leave. So people stay here, and people just die."

Virgil opened his mouth to respond, but Simon grabbed the key, jammed it to the left, popped open the door, jumped into the driver's seat, fired up the engine, and pulled through the parking spot, the Pontiac gasping for breath as it tore across the lot and pulled out into the midday city traffic, heading west.

Virgil stared after the car, spreading his arms open wide in disbelief. "But you're my ride," he said.

Simon did not come back.

CHAPTER 2

Simon pulled into the parking lot, a wide rectangle of dull white rocks. He threw the Pontiac into park. He turned off the ignition. He took a breath.

He got out of the car.

After three years, he knew the way to Laura's grave by heart.

He padded across the soft, uneven grass of the cemetery, passing tombstones that dated back to the 18th century. Templar had been one of the first towns settled in Pennsylvania, in the foothills of the Appalachians. There was a time when it had been on track to become the biggest city in the state; then Pittsburgh hit its steel boom and sapped some of its strength. But there was more history here, and with that history came the graveyards, with their roughly settled earth.

Simon pushed on through the older stones and headed up the hill, toward the newer section. He found Laura's grave right where he'd left it a few weeks before: at the end of the row, next to the rusty chain fence, overlooking Gossamer Lake.

He sat down on the grass and crossed his legs. Graveyards made some people uncomfortable, but not Simon. He had always been comfortable with the idea of the dead—not with death, but with the notion that people die, and that's how it goes.

He actually took comfort in the quiet of the cemetery. It was peaceful.

"Hey, Laura," he said, moving his eyes over the etching on her stone. *Laura Dark, Beloved Daughter and Sister*. The date of her death was carved near the bottom, six years ago to the day. Six years since they'd lost her. Six years that had gone by so fast.

Of course, the actual date was really just their best guess. On that autumn morning, Laura hadn't come down for breakfast. Their mother had gone upstairs to wake her up, and Simon could still remember the sound of her panic when she opened the door and found Laura's room empty. The bed hadn't been slept in.

Laura didn't come home that day, or the next day, or the next. The police had been notified, search parties had been sent out, but no one ever saw Laura again. What they *did* find was her bracelet, a thin chain with a silver charm shaped like an ice cream cone. Someone from one of the search parties had found it in the woods outside of city limits. It sat in the bottom of a circular pit that had been dug into the earth.

Pieces of Laura's skin had rubbed onto the silver of the chain. The coroner said that was a sign of a struggle. They tested the DNA, just to be sure it was her.

Laura was gone.

"Mom can't make it today," Simon said, blinking back his tears. "I mean, she *can* come, but she won't, or doesn't think she'd be able to, or whatever. She's not coming. And Dad... well, you know about Dad. I don't know if he even knows you're gone."

He caught some movement out of the corner of his eye, and he turned. Standing on the other side of the chain was Virgil. He was breathing hard from his climb up the hill, and his shaggy brown hair was blowing in the wind.

"When did you get here?" Simon asked.

"Just now," Virgil panted. "I would've been here sooner, but my ride just sort of left me in the parking lot. I had to take two buses, and then run up this stupid hill." He started to cross over the chain, but stopped. "Can I join you?" he asked first. Simon nodded, and Virgil stepped over the fence. "It's creepy here," he said, looking around.

"It's quiet."

"It's *too* quiet." He reached down and touched the top of the tombstone. "Hi, Laura."

"Sorry I left you at Squeezy Cheez," Simon said.

Virgil shrugged. "Hey, I didn't mean to make you mad. I know today's the anniversary. But that's, like, *why* we should do this. Because of Laura. Because of what happened to her."

"We don't know what happened to her," Simon pointed out.

"Exactly. We don't know what happened, but we know it was something evil. It might have even been Mrs. Grunberg's demon."

"It wasn't Mrs. Grunberg's demon," Simon said, rolling his eyes. "And we don't even know for sure that Mrs. Grunberg even *has* a demon."

"So let's go find out. And if she *does* have a demon, let's send it back to hell."

Simon snorted. He shook his head, but said nothing.

"Look," Virgil continued, sitting down on the grass next to Laura's grave. "How many people in Templar have disappeared like Laura did? How many people have died, or vanished, because there was no one to fight for them? We could be the ones who fight for them! We could be the ones who fight the monsters!"

"Are you even listening to yourself?" Simon asked, incredulous. "We can't *fight monsters,* Virgil!"

"We can't fight monsters *yet*," Virgil correct him. "But I have a plan."

He opened his mouth to elaborate, but Simon raised a hand, silencing him. "Hey," he said, his eyes suddenly alert. "Do you hear that?"

Virgil cocked his head to the side and strained his ears. At first, he didn't hear anything...but then, there it was: a soft, muffled sound, like it was coming from beneath a heavy blanket. It was the muted sound of something scratching on wood. "Actually, I do," he said. He crossed behind Laura's stone, careful not to step on the grave. Unlike Simon, he was a little more cautious about the dead.

He walked between the graves, listening carefully. The sound grew louder as he zeroed in on its source, and it changed, too. The scratching was interrupted by a hard cracking of wood...which transitioned into a gentle rumble. Virgil stepped up behind a tombstone four spots over from Laura's grave. He looked back at Simon and held a finger to his lips. He pointed down with his other hand. *This one.*

Simon nodded, and he pulled himself up from his seat on the ground. He crossed cautiously over to the grave, stepping lightly. "What is it?" he whispered, but Virgil shushed him.

They stared at the ground. It began to pulse from beneath, mounding up and sinking back down, up and down, like something was pushing up from under the earth.

Then a gray, mottled hand broke through the dirt, and Virgil began to scream.

CHAPTER 3

"Undead!" Virgil screeched. He lunged forward and knocked Simon back, pushing him out of the way, which was ultimately unnecessary, since the creature in the ground was having a slow time of crawling up from his grave.

"Get off!" Simon cried, pushing Virgil to the side. They leapt to their feet and turned to face the grave. The sickly hand had broken all the way through the earth, waving wildly from the elbow. The rotting fingers of a second hand had pushed up through the hole and were clawing at the earth, making the hole gap.

"Have you ever fought a zombie?" Virgil asked, his voice high and tight with fear.

"Of course I've never fought a zombie...I've never even *seen* a zombie!" Simon snapped.

"We saw that one in science class in fourth grade," Virgil reminded him.

"That one didn't count. It was in captivity."

The zombie pushed its other hand through the ground and clawed frantically at the grass, pulling more dirt down onto himself and pushing the hole out even wider. Soon its head rose through the clumps of earth and grass. The undead monster had once been a man. Now it was something else entirely.

It gasped for breath, the yellow-gray flesh hanging from its cheekbones, flapping open so they could see its teeth behind the skin. Its pupils were dull black, and the whites of its eyes had filmed over with a rotten yellow mucous. It coughed and snarled as it struggled up out of its grave, thick drips of saliva trailing from its lips.

"I don't remember anything from that class," Virgil realized. "How are you supposed to kill them?"

"How are you supposed to kill them? You go for the brain—have you never watched a movie?!" Simon demanded. "You always go for the brain!"

"Great," said Virgil, tracking the zombie's struggling movements. "Go for it with what?"

Simon looked around. "Maybe with a rock?"

"Do you see any rocks?"

"I don't see any *anything*."

"Use your foot," Virgil decided. "You can stomp on it with your foot."

"I'm not stomping on it with my foot!" Simon cried. "*You* stomp on it with *your* foot!"

"You're closer," Virgil pointed out.

"I'm not smashing in its brain with my foot!"

The zombie shrugged its shoulders out of the hole. It looked at Simon and Virgil with such blunt desire, with such *hunger*, that they both shuddered at the same time. The zombie planted its hands on the grass and pushed, hauling itself out of the grave.

"Too late now!" Simon said. He grabbed Virgil's sleeve and pulled him back. "We should go."

"Go? Go where?" Virgil asked, watching the zombie pull its legs out of the hole.

"Anywhere!"

"There's a school across the street!" Virgil cried. "We're just going to run away and let him have a middle school buffet for lunch?"

Simon gritted his teeth. He'd forgotten about the school. He stepped backward as the zombie clamored to its feet and took two uneasy steps on shaky, rotting legs. He peeked over the hill, down toward the section of the graveyard that sloped down to the lake. There was a blue tarp on the ground in the distance, covering a half-dug grave.

"I have an idea," he said. "Keep it busy." Then he turned and sprinted off in the direction of the lake, jumping over the chain and running down the hill.

"Keep it busy?" Virgil said, incredulous. "Keep it busy how?!" But Simon was out of earshot. "Great," he mumbled miserably. The zombie had found its footing. It lurched forward, throwing out its hands. It had a surprisingly long reach, and Virgil cried out as the creature's fingers brushed against his shirt. He stumbled backward, falling down onto the grass behind him. The zombie threw itself forward, snarling and slavering. It collapsed on top of Virgil, gnashing its teeth, reaching out for bites of his flesh. The zombie smelled like putrid death, and Virgil gagged as rotten skin and flecks of thick mucus flew into his mouth. He threw up his forearms, blocking the monster's teeth by holding back its throat. The creature was surprisingly strong; Virgil gasped for breath as he worked to hold the thing back. His arms began to press into the soft flesh, and then he felt something warm and wet spread down across his wrists. He looked up and almost vomited when he saw that his arms had pushed themselves straight through the zombie's skin, and its throat was leaking blood and saliva.

"Oh, gross!" Virgil moaned. He managed to get his feet up under the monster's ribcage, and he pushed off as hard as he could. The zombie flew up into the air, its arms and legs flailing like shredded pinwheels, and Virgil rolled out of the way just as it crashed back down onto the ground. Virgil scrabbled away on his hands and knees, heading toward the older graves.

The zombie pushed itself to its feet and stumbled after him, gasping and snarling. Virgil jumped up and jogged forward, laboring for breath. He hurried down the hill and spied a tall gravestone, a pillar with a stone angel perched on top. He ran around the grave marker and nudged it with his shoulder. It was heavy, and solid, but it swayed just a bit at his touch.

The zombie lumbered closer, slipping and sliding down the grass, moving faster than Virgil would have expected. It wasn't the slow, shuffling gait like in the old horror movies; this zombie stalked forward on jerky legs, his pace the regular walking pace of a human. It closed the gap quickly, and soon it was close enough for Virgil to smell the stench of it again.

He reared back, then jammed his shoulder forward, hitting the concrete pillar so hard that something in his elbow popped. The tombstone rocked forward, and the angel on top wobbled a little, but that was it. The zombie swiped its ragged fingers at Virgil, and he danced back, out of reach, and spun around the pillar, keeping the tower between himself and the zombie. He faked left, and the zombie dove, snarling. Virgil jerked himself back to the right, gave himself enough room for a running start, then sprinted forward, giving a throaty battle cry as he smashed into the concrete pillar with every ounce of force he could muster. The pillar swayed, and the angel on top tipped forward and balanced perilously on the edge of its base...then it fell forward, toppling head over heels as the zombie lurched forward.

The angel landed with a hard *thud* in the soft earth just to the left of the undead creature.

"Aw, come on," Virgil whimpered.

The zombie lunged again, and this time, he caught the hem of Virgil's shirt. The monster reared back its rotting head, exposing the hole that Virgil's arms had made in its throat. It snapped its head forward, teeth open and gnashing toward Virgil's arm.

Then the broad side of a metal shovel blade caught the zombie in the side of the head, sliced through the flesh, and stuck into the skull with a soft, wet *thump*.

The zombie fell over, dead. This time, for good.

"Took you long enough," Virgil groaned.

Simon shrugged, out of breath. "That hill is *really* steep." He tossed the shovel to the ground and helped Virgil to his feet. "You okay?"

"I had it under control," he said, brushing the grass from his pants.

"Yeah, it sure looked like it," Simon said.

"Hey, it wouldn't have been a problem if you had just stomped on it like I told you to."

"No way," Simon said, shaking his head. "These shoes are brand new."

They stood over the ruined body of the zombie. Virgil nudged it with the toe of his sneaker, just to make sure it was dead. "If the dead are going to start rising more often, we should bury them with air fresheners," he said, making a sour face.

"Almost makes me glad there was nothing left of Laura to bury," Simon said. Virgil gave him a questioning look. "I just…wouldn't want to think of her breaking down like that. You know?"

"Yeah," Virgil said, nodding. "I know."

Simon scratched his chin. "Does it seem weird to you? A demon *and* a zombie, both in Templar at the same time?"

"You know, I think most people would say either a demon *or* a zombie was pretty weird," Virgil said. He sighed. "Do you ever think that we should move to a normal city?"

But Simon waved this away. "No, I mean, think about it. This sort of thing has been happening a lot more often lately. That serpent in the lake just last month, and then a demon a few weeks later, now a zombie, too? We used to get *maybe* one weird thing a year." He frowned down at the zombie's lifeless body. "What's happening here?"

Virgil chewed his bottom lip. "You think something's happening?"

Simon raised an eyebrow. "Don't you?"

"I don't know. It *is* weirder than usual, so much happening so close together."

"It's never been like this before."

They stood quietly for a few minutes, each of them lost in thought. Slowly, a smile broke across Virgil's face. "So are you thinking what I'm thinking?"

Simon shook his head, and he sighed. "You know, Virg... I've got a bad feeling that I am, in fact, thinking what you're thinking."

Virgil looked at Simon. Simon looked at Virgil.

Together, in perfect unison, they said, "Templar needs some heroes."

CHAPTER 4

"This is so exciting!" Virgil hissed in Simon's ear.

Simon elbowed him, nudging him back. "Will you stop saying that?" he said. "And be quiet. And it's *not* exciting, it's terrifying. And be quiet!"

They were crouched in the alley across from Mrs. Grunberg's house, hiding from the streetlights of Evergreen Street in the shadow of the oversized dumpster. It had been thirty-six hours since they had taken down the zombie in the graveyard. Simon had spent most of those hours wondering why in the world he had agreed to become an amateur monster hunter. "I must be out of my mind," he mumbled.

"What you are is a solid eight percent cooler today than you were yesterday," Virgil said cheerfully.

"Remind me again why we think this stuff will work to take down an immortal spawn of Satan?" Simon said, inspecting the contents of their duffel bag for the fifth time since leaving their apartment. They had packed a box of Crayola chalk, a thick red candle, a lighter, four bottles of Jolt cola, a cylinder of Morton sea salt, and a length of nylon rope.

"Because the internet said so," Virgil said, like it was the most obvious thing in the world. "The internet knows everything."

"The internet thinks David Bowie was an undercover Colombian spy," Simon said.

"Can you prove that he wasn't?" Virgil asked, prodding Simon on the shoulder. "Huh? Go on, I dare you. Prove that he wasn't."

"You are such an idiot." He zipped up the bag and peered out from behind the dumpster. Mrs. Grunberg's house was an old Tudor-style mansion with a small yard nestled between two five-story apartment buildings. It looked completely out of place on the city block, with its sharply peaked roof and dark brown timber trim. A few wide flagstones served as a path from the sidewalk to the front porch steps. The front edge of the elevated porch was covered by white latticework, designed to hide the crawlspace beneath the floorboards of the porch. Normally, the space behind the latticework was dark. But for the past couple of weeks, a dark red light had been pulsing out through the small basement windows. The pulses made it look like a visual heartbeat, or a slow, dangerous breath.

There could have been any number of non-supernatural explanations for the weird light. But that wasn't the only change to the Grunberg house. The flowers in the small gardens lining either side of the house had all turned black. They hadn't died; they weren't shriveled or flaking away, losing their leaves or petals. They stood as strong as ever. They had just turned black. And every day, the darkness of the flowers seemed to grow thicker, and *wetter*. As they watched now, from across the street, Simon could swear that the black begonias were actually dripping.

"Definitely a sign of a demon," Virgil whispered, reading Simon's thoughts. "The internet confirmed it."

"What would a demon want with Mrs. Grunberg's basement?" Simon wondered aloud.

"Probably some peace and quiet," Virgil said. "Grunberg probably doesn't have Alexa or internet or anything. She's *super* old."

"Demons don't just appear," Simon muttered. "They're summoned. And they don't usually stay in one place, unless they're somehow trapped there."

"Oh, two days ago you're not ready to be a monster hunter, today you're a demon expert?" Virgil said, rolling his eyes.

Simon was suddenly grateful for the darkness behind the dumpster; it hid the fact that his face had turned pink with embarrassment. "I...read it on the internet," he admitted.

"Boy, what did people do before wi-fi?" Virgil wondered.

"They went to the library."

"Ew."

Simon exhaled. "I'm just saying, we might have bigger problems than a demon."

Virgil screwed up his face in confusion. "Like what?"

"Like someone with enough knowledge and strength to conjure up and control that demon."

Virgil considered this. "Hmm," he said thoughtfully, ticking his head back and forth. "Old lady Grunberg *has* been doing pilates..."

Simon gave him a look. "How do you even know that?"

Virgil smiled smugly. "I pay attention."

Simon turned and sat down on the cracked asphalt with his back leaning against the dumpster. "All right. Let's go through the plan one more time."

"We've been through the plan eighty thousand times," Virgil moaned, pressing his hands against the sides of his head in misery.

Simon looked over at him, his bright blue eyes as serious as death. "Then let's make it eighty-thousand-and-one."

"Okay, okay." Virgil crouched down and planted a finger on the ground. "This is the house." He drew his finger around in a wide circle. "We run over, we open the salt, and we pour it in a circle around the house."

"An *unbroken* circle," Simon clarified.

"Yes, an unbroken circle. A ring of salt should keep the demon from escaping, because I guess demons are more of a sweet tooth kind of monster."

"This is assuming the demon *wants* out, or is *able* to get out," Simon reminded him. "I'm telling you, it's not natural for it to just camp out there without being trapped and controlled."

"I know, I know, you asked Jeeves, and now you're a genius. The salt is there as a safety net, just in case it *does* try to run."

"Okay," Simon nodded. "Then what?"

"Then we do recon. Look through the windows and see what we can see."

"Try to assess what type of demon it is."

"Sure, I guess," Virgil shrugged. "I don't know why it matters."

"I'd like to know if it has horns, or hooves, or if it breathes fire, or has razor claws. I'd like to know what we're dealing with, exactly."

"It's a creature from hell, Simon, it's not going to have a whole lot of soft surfaces."

"We assess what type of demon it is," Simon said, getting them back on track. "See what we can see."

"Yes. We see what we can see, and we scope the layout of the basement, you find the best way in, and we make a plan of attack. Then we sneak in, head downstairs, light the candle, and say the magic protection words so the thing can't touch us."

"You brought the words?" Simon asked.

Virgil held up his phone. "All loaded up," he said.

"Remind me which website you found those on?"

"PurgeYourEvil.org."

"Great," Simon moaned. "Sounds really legit."

"Dude, it's a dot-*org*," Virgil said. "It's for real."

"Okay," Simon said, rolling his head on his neck and shaking out his hands, "okay. We pour the salt, scope the room, get inside, light the candle, say the words, face the demon, do the binding thing with the rope, draw the runes on the floor, say the purging spell, and if somehow the demon doesn't roast us with his fire breath or melt us with some acid vision along the way, that *should* send it back to hell."

Virgil looked at him, confused. "What is acid vision?"

Simon grimaced. "Let's hope we don't have to find out. And you're *sure* Mrs. Grunberg isn't home?"

"Does it look like she's home?" Virgil asked, gesturing over at the house. Aside from the pulsing red glow, there were no lights on in the entire place. "It's Monday. On Mondays, she plays bridge."

"How do you even—"

"I'm telling you, I pay attention!"

Simon's hands were slick with sweat. He rubbed them on his jeans. "So I guess that's it."

Virgil clapped his hands. "I feel good about this plan. Do you feel good about this plan?"

"I do not feel good about this plan, no."

"Great," Virgil said, jumping up to his feet. "Now let's go be heroes."

CHAPTER 5

There was an unmistakable heat emanating from beneath the house. Virgil could feel it radiating through his clothes, giving his skin a sickly warmth. "Gross," he muttered.

Pouring the salt in an unbroken ring was harder than it seemed. For one thing, Mrs. Grunberg had a fence encircling her backyard, with a locked gate, so Virgil had to climb over the fence to make it all the way around the house. The fence also made it challenging to make the circle unbroken; he had to toss salt beneath the slats of wood to bring the line into the backyard.

For another thing, there were a lot of plants around the house with wide leaves and sharp barbs. He tried pouring the salt down onto the plants, hoping it would rain down onto the ground thickly enough to continue the unbroken line, but the leaves were like umbrellas, scattering the grains of salt in all directions. So he had to push the plants down in order to draw the salt circle along the ground, and the thorns cut at his hands.

By the time he made it to the backyard, he was sweating, bleeding, and annoyed.

And, of course, the throbbing red glow from the basement was ever-present. He tried to complete his job quietly, and without drawing the attention of the demon, but at one spot in the backyard, where the storm windows were bigger than the thin glass plates along the sides of the house, he couldn't help himself, and he peeked inside.

The basement was mostly empty, except for a few stacks of weathered cardboard boxes in the corner, full of old clothes and Christmas decorations. There was a furnace, a hot water heater, and an old utility sink that was covered in cobwebs and looked like it hadn't been used in decades. The concrete floor was covered in dust...and there, in a high-backed wooden chair in the center of the room, sat the demon.

The creature was facing away, so Virgil couldn't get a good look at him. He was huge; that much was obvious. His shoulders rose high above the back of the chair like bulbous mountains, and his knees were spread wide, and seemed to take up half the width of the room. The demon wore a suit that stretched to fit his massive frame so the only skin that showed through was on his hands and the back of his head. It was impossible to tell the color of his skin in the dark red light, but Virgil could see the texture of his hands. The demon was covered in scales, like a snake.

Virgil gasped out loud at the sight of him.

The demon turned his head, just a little.

Virgil rolled over and cowered behind a bush for a few long moments before he gathered up the courage to slide out from behind the bush and peek back into the basement.

The demon had turned to face the window Virgil was looking through.

"What are you doing?" Simon hissed.

Virgil nearly jumped out of his skin. "Don't sneak up on me!" he whispered back, slugging him on the arm.

"What are you doing?" Simon said again. "You're supposed to be drawing the circle!"

"I *am* drawing the circle! I just stopped for a look."

"Yeah, I looked too," Simon admitted, sounding guilty. "He's terrifying."

"He's huge!"

"I think we should leave."

"It won't help to come back later...demons don't sleep," Virgil said, though he was completely guessing.

"No," Simon said, shaking his head, "I think we should leave forever, and never come back."

"What?!"

"Virgil, you saw that thing! You can't honestly think we can take him!"

"There are two of us!" Virgil pointed out. "And only one of him!"

"This is insane."

"We can't leave, Simon. Who else would deal with it?" Virgil hissed.

"No one! Because we're the only idiots dumb enough to think we can fight a demon!"

"We don't have to *fight* him, we just have to *expel* him!"

"He is going to expel our bones from our skeletons!" Simon snapped.

"That doesn't make sense," Virgil pointed out. "If our skeletons lost their bones, they wouldn't be skeletons anymore."

But Simon just shook his head. "I can't, Virgil. I can't do this."

Virgil climbed up to his knees. He placed his hands on Simon's shoulders and gave him a hard look, staring directly into his eyes. "Simon. Listen to me. I'm scared too. Okay? I'm scared out of my *mind*. But someone has to do something. If someone had done something six years ago, Laura might still be alive. But no one did anything. Let's be the someone who *does* something."

Simon's eyes filmed over with tears. He brushed them away. When he spoke again, his voice was clouded and shaky. "What if the thing we do is get ourselves killed?"

Virgil shrugged. "Then I won't have to go to my shift at the plant tomorrow. And that doesn't sound so bad."

Simon closed his eyes. He pictured Laura—not as she looked the last time he had seen her, but as she might look now. If she had lived. If someone had done something.

"Okay," he said, swallowing hard and nodding his head. "Let's do it. Let's do something."

"Good," Virgil said. "Besides, it's going to be fine. We have PurgeYourEvil.org on our side."

"Great," Simon mumbled. "Hurry up and finish the circle. I'll keep looking for the best way in, but I'll be able to breathe normally again if I'm on the other side of a line he can't cross."

Virgil nodded. He rose to his feet, picked up the Morton's salt, and continued his path along the grass, climbing over the fence and continuing on around toward the front of the house.

From this close up, he noticed the begonias weren't dripping liquid; they were dripping shadows. The soft, opaque drops collected on the tips of the leaves, then they floated down like smoke, disappearing when they hit the ground with a soft *pfffth* sound. "That's freakin' weird," he mumbled.

He drew the circle up the side of the house and crossed back into the front yard. He shook out the last leg of salt, connecting his trail to where it had started, completing the full, unbroken circle.

Virgil stood back. He waited. He checked his watch. He frowned.

He had expected something to happen. A flash of light, maybe, or the sound of a lock being thrown—*something*. But there was nothing remarkable about it. It was just a circle of salt.

"Don't steer me wrong, PurgeYourEvil," he muttered to himself. "Simon's going to be *super* angry if this doesn't work."

"If what doesn't work?" said a soft, warbling voice from behind him. Virgil screamed and jumped, flailing his hands and throwing salt in all directions. He spun around and was confronted with a small, thin, elderly woman, her white hair knotted on top of her head, a knitted blue shawl wrapped tightly around her shoulders.

"Mrs. Grunberg!" Virgil cried, his heart hammering in his chest. "What are you doing home?"

Mrs. Grunberg adjusted the half-moon spectacles that perched on the end of her nose. She squinted through the lenses and said, "Is that Victor?"

"Virgil," he replied. "Virgil Matter. Do you remember me?"

"Oh, of course!" Mrs. Grunberg said, brightening a bit. "I thought your family moved to the suburbs."

"My parents did," Virgil said, willing his pulse to slow. The old woman had scared the daylights out of him. "I'm still here. I room with, um, Simon? Simon Dark? Do you remember him?"

"Of course, of course! My Robert used to watch you boys when you were little! How nice to see you."

"Thanks," Virgil said. Then he added, "Um, you too."

Mrs. Grunberg looked down at the Morton salt container in his hand. Then she peered down at the curved line of salt running across her lawn. "Can I help you with something, Victor?" she asked.

"It's Virgil. Um..." He looked down at the salt line, too. "I was...I'm just...it's that...you have...slugs," he lied.

Mrs. Grunberg frowned. "Slugs?"

"Yes, ma'am. Garden slugs. Big, *huge* garden slugs!" he said, really leaning into the lie. He held his hands two feet apart to show her how long they were. "Massive! And really dangerous. So I'm...um...salting. For the slugs."

Mrs. Grunberg smiled. "Oh, you are a dear," she said, patting his cheek. "Such a nice boy, helping out an old woman like me."

"Yes, ma'am," Virgil said, blushing.

"I'd invite you in for some milk, but I have so much to do!" she said, hobbling past Virgil and heading toward the porch stairs. She seemed oblivious to the red light pulsing out from under the porch. "My grandson Neil is coming tomorrow. He's been coming by a few times a week to help me around the house, and I need to make up the guest bed." She pulled herself up the stairs with the help of the handrail. She paused at the top of the porch and looked down at Virgil, squinting through her glasses. "Hmm," she said, looking him up and down. Her demeanor changed, and she wrinkled up her face, looking down at him with something like disappointment, or disdain. Maybe it was the fact that he was covered in dirt and sweat from the labor of drawing the circle around the house...or maybe she sensed something about him, felt his true motive. Maybe it wasn't that she hadn't noticed the red light from the basement, but that she had ignored it. Maybe she *had* conjured up the demon, and she sensed that Virgil had come to expel it. Or maybe it was just the dirt and the sweat. Whatever it was, she frowned down on him and said, "There's a sink in the basement. I leave the back door unlocked. Go on down there and wash up." It wasn't a question; it was a command.

A chill ran through Virgil's skin. "Yes, ma'am," he said, but his voice came out in a squeak.

Old Mrs. Grunberg nodded, then she turned back and walked up to the door. "Go down to the basement," she said again, pushing her key into the lock and opening the door. "I mustn't let you go home like that, when you've been so helpful to me."

Then she was inside the house, and she slammed the door shut.

CHAPTER 6

Virgil relayed the story of what had just happened with Mrs. Grunberg to Simon. "I think this might be a trap," Virgil said, out of breath from climbing back over the fence.

"Oh, you think?" Simon whispered, rolling his eyes.

"I'm just saying, we should be careful down there."

"That's a really good idea, because I was planning on smashing in through a window, running up to the demon, and punching him right in the face," Simon said sarcastically.

"Well I don't think *that's* a very good plan," Virgil pointed out. Simon sighed.

They approached the back door. It was a heavy wooden thing, set into the jamb with thick, rusty hinges. It looked like it belonged in a castle dungeon, not in the backyard of a Tudor-style mansion three blocks from a Starbucks in northwestern Templar.

"She said she keeps it unlocked," Virgil said, motioning toward the door.

"I know," Simon replied, "I checked it while you were drawing the circle." He looked down at the line of salt in front of his feet. "I guess if everything goes badly, we can just run back up here, right? Dive across the line, and be safe?"

"That's the plan," Virgil shrugged.

"All right," Simon said, nodding. "Better get your words ready."

Virgil slipped his phone out of his pocket and called up the website while Simon dug through the gym bag and pulled out the candle, the lighter, the chalk, and the rope. He slung the rope loop over his shoulder, and he took a piece of chalk from the box and pushed it into his back pocket so he wouldn't have to fumble with the box downstairs. He took out a second piece and handed it to Virgil, who tucked it behind his ear like a pencil.

"Can we light the candle out here, or do we have to be closer to the demon?" Simon asked.

"As long as we do it inside the circle, it should work," Virgil replied.

Simon took a deep breath. He closed his eyes. He stepped inside the circle.

"Why are you acting so weird? You already went up to the house, you already tried the door," Virgil pointed out.

"I know!" Simon snapped. "But now we're going *through* the door, and I'm nervous!" He knelt down on the grass, huddling against the candle to protect the flame, even though there wasn't much of a breeze. "Ready?" he asked. Virgil nodded. Simon flicked the lighter to life, and he held the flame to the wick.

The candle wouldn't catch fire.

"Why won't it light?" Simon hissed.

"I don't know...it's new! Sometimes it takes a while with a new wick!"

"You didn't pre-burn it?"

"Why would I pre-burn it? No, I didn't pre-burn it!"

"You always pre-burn it!" Simon said, annoyed. He clicked the lighter again, and this time he held the flame against the nylon wick until the wax melted away and the material caught fire. The small flame flickered orange and yellow in the darkness, cutting through the glow of red coming from the basement windows. Simon nodded at Virgil. "Go ahead," he said.

Virgil swiped up on the screen until he found the beginning of the spell. "Okay, here we go," he said. He took a deep breath. He looked at the words. Then he frowned. He cocked his head, and he squinted down at the screen.

"What's wrong?" Simon demanded.

"The spell is in Latin," Virgil whispered back. "I don't speak Latin."

"You're just now realizing that the spell is in Latin and that you don't speak Latin?!" Simon squeaked, trying to keep his voice down. His face flushed red with impatience. "Didn't you read this before coming out here?"

"I saw there was a spell, I didn't *read* the spell!" Virgil said. "I didn't want to use it up, in case it only works once!"

"You are *such* an idiot." Simon swiped Virgil's phone and shoved the candle into his friend's hands. The flame flickered and flattened, but it didn't go out. Simon zoomed in on the words. He had taken a semester of Latin in high school, mostly to impress a girl named Lisa who was also taking the class. But during the third week of the semester, he saw Lisa in the cafeteria holding hands with the captain of the lacrosse team. Latin lost all its luster after that. Simon hadn't been able to pay attention to a single lesson. Still, he had learned enough during those first few weeks to know how to pronounce most of the vowels. "Okay," he said, shaking out his shoulders. "Here goes nothing."

The spell was long, two full paragraphs, and Simon struggled through it. Some of the words, he knew, like *ignis* and *malum*...but others, like *praesidio* and *spatium*, he had to guess at. There was one passage that read, *Da mihi clypeus; da mihi solatium*. He had to read that one three times before he got it right. But Virgil kept nodding encouragingly, so he pressed on, reading the ancient words and, he hoped, weaving a passable spell of protection.

"*Ab hoc malo defendat*," he read, finishing the enchantment.

As soon as he said the word *defendat*, the flame of the candle roared to life, bursting into a huge tongue of fire, so large and hot that it singed Virgil's eyebrows. Virgil almost dropped the candle, but he recovered just before it slipped from his grasp, and they watched in open-mouthed wonder as the flame continue to burn high and wide, a softball of fire perched atop a stout red base. The colors of the flame flickered from yellow to orange to blue to red to green to purple, and then continued to burn blueish-purple as it slowly shrank and reformed itself into a normal-sized candle flame, dancing lazily on the wick.

"Two points for PurgeYourEvil.com," Virgil said, amazed.

"Not bad," Simon admitted, emboldened somewhat by the apparent success of the spell. "Did the salt do something weird when you completed the circle, too?"

"Yep," Virgil lied, nodding vigorously, "sure did."

"Okay," Simon replied, and for the first time all night, a smile crept across his face. His eyes shone with a newfound bravery. "Let's send this demon back to hell!"

They stood up, each holding the candle with one hand, and they crossed to the old basement door.

Simon turned the handle and pulled it open. The short stairwell was flooded with the pulsing blood-red light. He stepped onto the first stair, going sideways so he and Virgil could both hold the candle while they descended the steps.

When they were halfway down the stairwell, they heard a loud, deep laugh that shook the entire house. Then the door behind them slammed itself shut, and the entire cellar plunged into darkness.

CHAPTER 7

"What happened to the red light?" whispered Simon, alarmed. The purplish-blue candle flame still flickered in the dark, but it gave off only a dim, watery light, not enough to see by.

"I don't know," Virgil whispered back, and the fear in his voice was clear. "Maybe...we should go." He turned and grabbed the doorknob with his free hand, but it wouldn't turn. He shook the knob, pulling at the door, but the heavy thing only rattled in the doorjamb, and it would not give.

They were trapped.

"You're not leaving already?"

The voice of the demon enveloped them like a shroud. It was a smooth sound, thick and dense, as if the words themselves could swallow up any other sound that might try to exist in their space. Simon had the strange sensation that if he had some light, he would actually be able to *see* the words hanging in space, floating around them, squeezing their shoulders with their weight.

"Say something," Virgil whispered, giving Simon a nudge.

"*You* say something!" Simon hissed back.

"You're in front!"

"This whole thing was your idea!"

"Gentlemen," the demon interrupted, his voice billowing up from the darkness below like a heavy fog. It sounded as if it came from everyone and nowhere all at once. "Seeing as how we're all gathered here inside the circle, and each of us a bit trapped, why don't you come down so we can make proper introductions?" He breathed an indecipherable word from a long-dead language, and tiny orbs of red light filled the stairwell.

Each was the size of a firefly, and they hung in the air like stars, lighting the way to the cellar.

Virgil and Simon couldn't see the demon. He was still hidden in the shadows somewhere in the main area of the cold, damp room. "What do we do?" Virgil whispered.

Simon knew exactly what they would do. It was the only thing they *could* do. He tightened his grip on the candle. "We go down."

They stepped slowly down the stairs, pushing the red lights out of the way, holding the red candle between them. The flame seemed to diminish somewhat as they descended, shrinking back into itself bit by bit. But it didn't go out.

They reached the bottom of the stairs, their eyes still struggling to adjust to the utter darkness of the cellar. Simon pressed himself back against the wall, and Virgil followed suit, as if they could melt back into the cement and disappear if only they pushed hard enough.

"Step forward," the demon commanded.

And, having no other real alternative, they did.

They moved in the darkness, and as soon as they had taken two steps, the glare of the red light flamed back to life, and they squinted against the brightness of it. Once their eyes began adjusting to the glare, they peered into the basement room and saw the face of the demon for the first time.

At least, they saw the face the demon wanted them to see.

He sat in his high-backed chair, his right leg crossed over his left knee at the ankle, leaning back, with one arm slung back over the top of the chair. He wore a pressed white shirt under his gray suit, with the collar open at the throat. He wore shiny, black, expensive-looking loafers on his feet, with no socks. His skin was covered in a thin layer of scales, just as Virgil had noted from outside, but the glare of the pulsing red light was so strong that it was impossible to make out their color.

So instead, they looked at the demon's face, which was covered by a white porcelain mask. An elastic string was fixed to each side just above the cheekbones; it stretched over the demon's great head, holding the mask tightly in place. The porcelain reached as high as his forehead, and as low as his chin, but his head was too big to be completely covered, and skin and scales protruded from above and below. His scales seemed to climb up the sides of his neck, but to become thinner and more widely spaced as they went up his jaw. The dome of his head was a rough, scabby mess of sickly pale skin, like plastic that had been set on fire, then stretched over the top of a skull.

The porcelain mask was shaped like a baby's face, with squinting eyes, pursed lips, and big, puffed-up cheeks that were highlighted with soft pink paint that glistened through the enamel coating. A short tendril of hair had even been molded into the porcelain, swooping down in a Superman curl beneath the upper edge.

"This is the most scared I've ever been," Virgil whispered.

Simon was too terrified to reply.

The demon's left wrist rested against his propped-up knee, and he held his hand open, palm facing the ceiling. The pulsing red light seemed to emanate from that hand, though the exact source was indeterminable; he wasn't holding any sort of light, nor was the hand itself glowing. But the light was brightest around his palm; when it became lighter, the room became lighter, and when it grew darker, the room became darker. "Come closer," he said, his voice made soft by the porcelain, "and let us get to know each other."

"Here feels pretty good," Virgil piped up. He nudged Simon's shoulder.

"We're good here," Simon confirmed.

The demon uncrossed his legs. He leaned forward, placing his elbows on his knees, keeping the one hand open, and full of light. He tilted his head, as if considering them carefully. "I have not seen a Phoenician armament spell in many, many centuries," he mused. They could see his eyes behind the slits in the mask, and he was looking at the dark purple flame of their candle. "Though this one is inexpertly made."

"I only took one semester of Latin," Simon found himself explaining.

"The spell is in Phoenician," the demon countered. He scratched the underside of his chin. "The original was, at any rate."

Virgil caught Simon moving out of the corner of his eye. He watched as Simon slyly reached a hand into his back pocket and pulled up the edge of the piece of chalk that hid there. Simon looked at Virgil and raised an eyebrow. Virgil nodded; he had gotten the message. They had to see the plan through...which meant Simon would try to bind the demon with the rope while Virgil set to work on the chalk runes that would open the portal to the Anguish Dimension and send the demon back where it belonged. The only problem was that Virgil's chalk was behind his left ear. With his left hand gripping the candle, he couldn't reach up and grab the chalk without being obvious. If he had any chance of taking the chalk without the demon seeing, he would have to let go of the candle, or at the very least, he would have to switch hands, and he had no idea if that would break the spell or not. He had a hunch that it might.

At that point, Simon was realizing that he had an extremely similar problem. He had coiled the rope over his right shoulder, and he couldn't slip it off without letting go of the candle on *his* end.

They looked at each other. They sighed.

They weren't so great at planning.

"Introductions," the demon said, studying them from his chair in the center of the mostly-empty basement. He placed his free hand on his own chest. "I am Asag, lord of plague, commander of stone." He bowed his head deeply. "And you?"

"I'm Vir—" Virgil began, but Simon kicked him with the side of his shoe. "Ow!"

"Don't tell him your name!" Simon said, incredulous.

"Well, he told us his name!"

"So what?!"

"So I don't want to be rude!"

"*He's a demon!*"

Virgil thought about that for a second. "Well, that's true."

"No need," the demon Asag said, dismissing them with a wave of his hand. "You are known to me already, Virgil Matter. As are you, Simon Dark."

Simon started. "How do you know who we are?"

But the demon ignored the question. He stood up, and Simon and Virgil each instinctively took a step backward. At his full height, Asag's head nearly scraped the wooden struts that formed the ceiling overhead. Simon forced himself to stay on his feet, which was no easy task, since his knees had turned to jelly. Virgil watched in open-mouthed awe as the demon stretched, the gray cotton suit straining against his considerable bulk. "I'll admit, I am curious as to the nature of your visit," Asag said, and he took a step toward them. Simon gripped the candle tighter, and the flame seemed to grow just a bit larger. Asag noticed it, too; he stopped and tilted his head at the candle, staring at it through the holes in the porcelain baby mask. Then he took a step backward, keeping a safe distance. "Have you come to sacrifice yourselves to me?" he asked, sounding genuinely interested, as if that might be a perfectly good reason for them to be there.

"We came to send you back to hell!" Virgil cried. He spat at the demon. The mucous landed on Asag's shoe, where the demon's heat sizzled it away.

"What are you doing? You don't antagonize a demon!" Simon hissed.

"You have to project confidence, or he won't respect you," Virgil whispered back.

"He's a lord of plague, not a puppy!"

"Same rules apply!" Virgil snapped. "PurgeYourEvil.org!"

Asag cleared his throat, and the two men stopped bickering. "This is a different sort of visit, then," the demon decided. "I do not wish to be sent back to that realm. As such, your stated purpose puts us at odds." He motioned toward the stairwell, and the door at the top of the stairs burst open, slamming against the wall of the house. "Your magic is small," Asag continued, "and you reek of fear. I will allow one of you to leave, but the other shall be a sacrifice unto me."

"No way, Baby Mask," Virgil said, sounding so confident that Simon had to admit he was impressed. "We're here to see it through." He turned to Simon and nodded. "Templar needs heroes," he said.

Simon sighed. "Apparently it does."

They were agreed.

Then things began to happen very, very quickly.

Asag spread his shoulders wide, puffing himself up even larger, and lunged forward. The protection spell surrounding the two young men stopped him from getting too close, and the demon halted mid-air as if he had smashed into a glass plate. But the movement was enough to scare Simon, and he was frightened into action. He grabbed the candle with his left hand and let go with his right; mercifully, the spell held. Then he shook the rope down from his shoulder until the loop slid down onto his wrist. He reached into his back pocket with the fingertips of his right hand and grabbed the chalk. He pulled it out, stuck one end in his teeth, and used his free hand to tie the rope around the chalk.

"What are you doing?" Virgil asked, confused.

But Simon didn't answer. Instead, he pulled the knot tight, then handed that end of the rope to Virgil. "Take it!" he said.

Virgil frowned down at the chalk. "It was in your mouth," he pointed out.

"*Take it!*"

Virgil did as he was told, making a sour face. Asag was pacing in front of them now, obviously irritated by the strength of their protection spell. Their magic might have been small, but it was sufficient...for now. But there was no way of knowing how long it would hold. Already, the flame had burned through more than half of the candle.

"Throw it around him," Simon instructed.

Virgil blinked. "What?"

"The rope—throw it around him!"

"It's not a boomerang, Simon!"

"The chalk gives it weight, whip it around him, it'll come around! Like tether ball!"

"Oh!" Virgil said, brightening. "Got it!" Without letting go of the candle, he shook out a length of the rope with his right hand, making sure Simon still had a tight hold of the other end. He began to spin the chalk end like a lasso. The demon moved, skirting to his left, trying to get out of reach, but Simon and Virgil instinctively moved as one unit, carrying the protection spell together and blocking the demon's progress. Virgil sensed his moment, and he let the rope fly. The piece of chalk sailed past Asag, and the rope caught him just above the elbow. The weight of the chalk carried the rope behind him and swung back around the far side of the demon, hitting the floor near Simon's shoe. The demon tried to dance out of the rope, but Simon lurched down, picked up the chalk, and yanked the rope back up before Asag could step over it.

Simon exhaled, allowing himself a moment of pride.

They had lassoed a demon.

"I'll bind, you draw!" Simon hollered, taking the end of the rope between his teeth and snatching the other end from Virgil's right hand. He set to work making a loop, and as he did so, he recited the words of the binding spell. *Those* words were easy; they were in English. "I bind you; I bind you; I bind you," he said, his mouth full of rope. The demon groaned like he was in pain. "Virgil!" Simon said with his teeth clenched on the rope. "Draw!"

"Okay!" Virgil reached up for the chalk that was perched behind his ear, but the angle was awkward, his right hand going to his left ear, and he accidentally pushed the chalk back. It fell from behind his ear and clattered to the ground, breaking into three pieces. He panicked, and he reached down to grab the chalk...but he reached with his left hand, letting go of the candle.

The protection spell was broken.

The flame fizzed and sputtered like it might go out. When it got ahold of itself and flared back to life, the purplish hue had drained from it, and the tongue of fire was once again yellow. Simon and Virgil both stared at the candle, stunned. Asag's expression was impossible to read behind the mask...but he stepped forward, bent down, lowered his face to the flame, and blew out the candle.

"Okay, wait—" Virgil started to plead, holding his hands up in helplessness, but the demon reached out, pressed his mammoth, scaly hand to Virgil's chest, and whispered something in his ancient language. Virgil felt something warm spread through his chest, and then the air rushed out of him, as if it were being sucked out of his spine by a vacuum cleaner, and he looked at Simon with sad, pleading eyes. "I'm sorry," he whispered. Then there was a popping sound, and just like that, Virgil was gone, sucked away into nothingness.

"*Virgil!*" Simon screamed. He dropped the candle and rushed forward, hands outstretched, into the space where his best friend had just been standing. But there was nothing but empty air.

Simon's jaw hung open. He turned to face the demon. "What did you do?" he asked, momentarily forgetting his fear. He raised his voice and asked again, louder, more angrily, "*What did you do?*"

Asag stepped out of the circle of rope, which lay sadly and unimpressively on the dusty concrete floor. "The next time you attempt a binding spell, I suggest you don't do it with your mouth full," he said, advancing on Simon. The light from his hand grew dimmer, the room became darker. "Correct enunciation is important." Then the demon closed his open palm, and the light was fully extinguished.

Simon was plunged into darkness with the devil.

CHAPTER 8

Virgil opened his eyes. "Am I dead?" he asked aloud.

He didn't receive an answer, which he took as a bad sign. The space around him was dark and blurred, just a mess of black and gray shapes swimming together in the air. But as he blinked, the shapes began to form into sharp curves and lines, and color began to bleed into his vision, and soon the world was reforming before him. The shapes above him were leaves. The thing beyond that was a streetlamp. And the darkness beyond that was sky.

Virgil sat up, and his head rushed with pain. He squeezed his eyes shut and inhaled sharply through his teeth, placing his hand against his forehead until the pain subsided into a dull throb. He opened his eyes again, and he saw that he was sitting in Mrs. Grunberg's front yard. Everything looked as it had before: the begonias still dripped with black shadows, the ring of salt was still spread across the grass, and the house was still dark. Actually, the house was *too* dark. *That* was something that had changed: the pulsing red light had gone out.

There was nothing but cold, empty darkness beneath the porch.

"Simon!" he screamed. He scrambled to his feet, but they were sluggish in responding. His knees buckled as he lurched forward, and he crashed back down to the ground on his chest. He pushed himself back up, and he coaxed his body forward, stumbling across the grass toward the backyard fence. As he shuffled past the dark begonias, something melted forward out of the darkness, and he cried out in surprise, skidding to a stop.

It was Simon. He had appeared in the side yard as if he had passed straight through the wooden slats of the fence.

"Simon!" Virgil cried, stumbling forward. He threw an arm around his friend's shoulder and guided him back toward the front of the house. "Are you okay? What happened?" Simon was as white as a sheet. The color had completely drained from his skin, except for the dark purple circles that had swollen up beneath his eyes. He was unfocused, staring out toward the street, staring at nothing, and he walked with his arms hanging straight down and unmoving at his sides. "Simon? Come on, talk to me," Virgil said, snapping his fingers in front of Simon's face.

After a few snaps, Simon shook his head, like he was clearing something out of it, and he looked at Virgil as if seeing him for the first time. "Oh. Virgil?" he asked, screwing up his face and sounding confused.

"Yeah, buddy, it's me. Hey, are you okay?" Virgil pulled Simon out onto the sidewalk, under the streetlight, and inspected him more closely. Simon's skin was clammy, and his blond hair was matted down with sweat. "What happened?" he asked again. He looked back at the house. The basement was still dark. "Simon, did you—did you kill the demon?"

Simon stared back at his friend, his eyes huge. And when he spoke again, his voice was an empty, hollow whisper: "He took off the mask."

"What?"

"He...took off the mask." A single tear spilled over the corner of Simon's eye. It rolled down his cheek and dripped onto the sidewalk. He turned slowly away from Virgil and began shuffling down the sidewalk, back in the direction of their apartment.

"Hey!" Virgil said as he ran to catch up. "Hey! Simon! What happened?! Are you okay?" He snapped his fingers in front of Simon's eyes again, and Simon swatted him away. He didn't stop walking. Virgil jumped in front of him, grabbed him by the shoulders, and gave him a good shake. "Simon! *What happened?!*"

Simon stopped. He looked at Virgil, really *looked* at him, focusing on his eyes, and he looked startled as if he just realized Virgil was standing there. "Asag put something inside of my head," he said simply. Then he squirmed out of Virgil's grasp and continued walking toward home.

Virgil followed closely behind, prodding him with more questions, but Simon was too shell-shocked to speak, and he stumbled the rest of the way in silence.

As they rounded the corner, out of sight of old Mrs. Grunberg's house, the basement windows began to pulse with red light.

CHAPTER 9

"Well, that did *not* go well," Virgil said with a frown.

"No," Simon sighed, taking a sip of his Dr. Pepper. He swallowed it down. "No, it did not."

They were sitting at a table at Squeezy Cheez, poking at pieces of a sausage pizza, neither of them particularly hungry. Their regular table, the one over by the Skee-Ball area, had been claimed by a ten-year-old's birthday party, and they were forced to sit closer to the register, where the smell of popcorn was stifling. Virgil hated the smell of popcorn. Every few minutes, he shot a glare over toward the children sitting in their place.

"So what happened to you last night?" Virgil asked, taking a bite of his pizza. The grease dribbled onto his shirt, but he ignored it; he had just come from his shift at the ball bearing plant, and the cheese grease blended in perfectly with the machine grease on his blue, short-sleeved, button-down work shirt. Even the white patch on his chest with "Signal Bearings" embroidered in red letters was covered in grime.

"Do you ever wash your shirt?" Simon asked.

Virgil shrugged. "I have before." He glowered at the children across the room. One of the kids stuck her tongue out at him in response.

Simon sank back into his plastic chair. He fiddled with his soda cup, flicking it with his fingers. "I don't know exactly what happened," he admitted. "I don't remember much."

"That's kind of weird, right?" Virgil asked with his mouth full. "Aren't people supposed to remember trauma?"

"I think people are supposed to *bury* their trauma."

"That doesn't sound healthy."

"No, I don't mean they're *supposed* to do it, I mean, supposedly, that's what—look, who cares, I'm just saying, I don't remember much."

"What *do* you remember?" Virgil asked, leaning forward with interest. "You said Asag put something inside your head."

"I remember you disappearing when he touched you. I mean, you *vanished*." Simon looked at his friend, his eyes wide with the shock of the memory. "You were there, then you were gone, like *that*." He punctuated this by snapping his fingers. "I thought you were vaporized. I thought you were *dead*."

"That makes two of us," Virgil muttered. "I was in the basement, then I was in Grunberg's front yard, and there was just a whole lot of nothing in-between."

"Why would he just...send you away like that?" Simon wondered.

Virgil shrugged. "Demons gotta demon," he said, chomping down on his pizza.

Simon snorted. He placed his palms flat on the table. "After that," he said, "things get sort of fuzzy. He told me to speak more clearly when I say my spells. I do remember that."

"Yeah, I didn't want to say anything, but you really shouldn't try to do magic with your mouth full," Virgil said with his mouth full.

Simon pressed on, ignoring him. "Then he put out the light. And..." He closed his eyes and took a deep breath. "And then I don't remember anything after that. I don't even remember getting home."

Virgil raised an eyebrow as he sipped on his Orange Slice. "Really? Nothing?"

"Nothing from when it went dark until I woke up this morning."

"Huh. That's weird."

"Why?"

"Because last night, when you...I don't know, *emerged* from the basement, when I found you near the side of the house, you said something weird. You said, 'He took off the mask.'"

Simon wrinkled his nose in confusion. "I did?"

"Yeah. You were as white as this," Virgil said, holding up his wadded napkin. Then he looked down at it. "Well. Whiter than this. As white as this was before it got pizza all over it." He tossed the napkin onto the table in disgust.

"I don't remember any of it," Simon shrugged. "Really."

Virgil shifted uncomfortably in his seat. "Well...do you think he...*did* anything to you?"

"What do you mean, 'anything'? Like what?"

"Like I don't know, like...maybe he...put something inside of you?"

Simon narrowed his eyes. "Why are you asking me that?"

Virgil squirmed again, visibly uncomfortable. "It's just... you also sort of said that he put something inside your head."

"I did?" Simon started.

Virgil nodded. "Yeah."

Simon moved his head around on his shoulders. It didn't feel any different than usual. He held out his arms and looked down, giving himself a visual inspection. He flexed his fingers, and he flexed his toes. Everything seemed fine. "I don't *think* he put anything inside of me," he said with a frown.

"Well, I guess we'll find out soon enough," Virgil said, scooting back his chair. "If he did, you are *not* going to stay healthy."

"Great, thanks," Simon said miserably. He watched as Virgil hopped to his feet. "Where are you going?"

Virgil looked at him like it was the stupidest thing he'd ever heard. "Dude. Skee-Ball."

"Are you serious? You tell me a—" He realized how loud he was being, and he remembered the children a few tables over. He lowered his voice to a whisper. "You tell me a demon showed me his face and then put something inside my head, and then you leave to go play *Skee-Ball?*"

Virgil shrugged. "Yeah. Dude. I need that Nerf gun." He scoffed and walked away, heading toward the token machine.

"Unbelievable," Simon murmured to himself. He picked up a piece of pizza and studied it, trying to decide if he was hungry enough to take a bite. He hadn't eaten anything all day. The events of the night before—the ones he could remember, anyway—had shaken him enough that he'd lost his appetite. Add to that the things he *couldn't* remember, and Simon wasn't sure he'd ever want to eat again. He gave up and tossed the slice of pizza back down onto the pan.

He heard a loud bang across the room, and he looked up to see Virgil whacking the side of the token machine with his open palm. "Come on, you stupid thing!" Virgil cried, smacking the metal box again. "*Why won't you work?*"

A few of the kids at the birthday table giggled.

"Virgil, just go up to the counter," Simon called across the room, but he was drowned out by the whirs and dings and buzzes and blips of a hundred arcade games, and by the sound of Virgil's own fury. He sighed and pushed himself up from the table, pulling his wallet from his pocket and walking toward the cash register himself.

Sometimes, when it came to Virgil, the easiest solution was the one that actually removed Virgil from the situation.

The new girl was working the counter. Her purple bob was pulled back into a tight, tiny ponytail, and she was wearing glasses today, big, thick-rimmed glasses with square lenses that magnified her green eyes, made them look huge, like a Disney character. She wore a silver locket around her neck, and a black zip-up hoodie that was two sizes too large over a red-and-white striped boat neck shirt. Her jeans were the expensive, stylish kind that looked brand new but had a ragged hole in the knee anyway, like they had come that way. They probably had.

Simon had never been this close to her before. She smelled like peppermint.

"Um, hi," he said, his voice shifting awkwardly. He gave her a wave, which he immediately regretted, because he was standing just eighteen inches away from her, on the other side of the counter. He winced. "Hi," he said again, and then he felt stupid for doing *that,* because he had already said it. He blushed.

The girl raised one perfect eyebrow, looking unimpressed. "Abby," she said.

"What?"

"Abby. When you say hi to a person, it's nice if you can finish with their name. So you should say, 'Hi, Abby.'"

"Oh. Your name is Abby," he said dumbly.

Abby blinked. "Yeah," she said.

Simon cleared his throat. "Great. Um." He coughed. This was not going well. "Hi. Abby. Um...my friend is..." He looked over at Virgil, who was physically assaulting the token machine, rocking it back and forth and yelling at it loudly enough to drown out the animatronic animal band that had just started its set in the next room. Simon frowned. "Well, he's...he's an idiot, I guess, and could I just get him some tokens?" He held up a ten-dollar bill.

Abby watched Virgil rocking the machine. "If he breaks it, he owes us, like, eighty thousand dollars."

"I think it's already broken," Simon pointed out.

Abby looked at him, unimpressed. "If he breaks it *more.*"

"Right. Got it," Simon said, nodding and swallowing hard. "Um, could I...get tokens, then?"

"Sure," Abby said, her voice wavering between sarcasm and irritability. She held out her palm. "Anyone can get anything if they have the cash."

Simon placed the bill in her hand. He meant to do it smoothly; he meant to do it casually. But there was something about Abby's eyes, magnified by her glasses...or maybe it was something about her hair, shining like a galaxy in the Squeezy Cheez fluorescent lights...or maybe it was something about her smell, which wasn't *just* peppermint, but peppermint lined with gingerbread and honey, he now noticed. Whatever it was, it caused his hand to tremble as he handed her the bill, and when he did, his fingertips brushed against the skin of her palm.

Abby cried out in pain. She yanked her hand back against her chest, cradling it like a broken bird, and reeled back, away from the counter. She fell against the far wall, her face given over to complete and total shock. She stared at Simon with wide, frightened eyes. And she just stood there, frozen in place, rooted by her fear.

Simon instinctively raised his hands in the air and backed away. "Are you okay? What? Are you—?" he cried, his eyes darting nervously. "What happened?"

Abby gasped, and her breath was coming fast now, her chest heaving in desperate attempts to pull in enough air fill her lungs. "Who *are* you?"

"I'm—I'm Simon," he sputtered. "Simon Dark. I—are you—are you okay?"

Abby placed a hand against her chest and closed her eyes. Her breathing began to slow. "No, I mean, who *are* you?"

Simon frowned. "I don't...I don't know what you mean," he said.

Abby opened her eyes. She stepped forward, planting both hands on the counter and leaning forward, staring hard at Simon. "I mean that there are two types of people who go around confronting demons, brave people and stupid people, and I need to know which one you are."

Simon started. "How did you know I confronted a demon?"

"I felt it," she said. She nodded at his hand. "When you touched me."

"How is that—"

"I'm an empath," she said curtly. She used a tone of voice that said she was sick of explaining this to people and would be all too happy never to have to do it again.

"You're an empath?" Simon asked. He felt an ember of excitement burn to life in the pit of his stomach. "A *real* empath?"

Abby rolled her eyes. "Yes, a real empath," she sighed. "When someone touches me, I can feel their feelings, and sometimes I can see their thoughts."

"No way."

"Yes way. I usually wear gloves that mostly block it out, because going through life taking on people's baggage is the absolute worst way to live. Trust me. But Squeezy Cheez says it's 'unprofessional' to wear gloves. But you know what?" She reached beneath the counter and pulled out a pair of gray elbow-length gloves. She pulled them on, flexing her fingers beneath the thin material. "They can go screw themselves, because it's bad enough handing change back to parents and taking on all their panic and stress for a few seconds, and if people like you are going to be coming in here, throwing a supernatural layer on top of everything, then they can deal with me being unprofessional, or they can find some other bored and totally disinterested drone to work the register."

Simon wasn't following any of this rant. He was still stuck on the whole "empath" thing. "You can see people's thoughts?" he asked.

"Yep. And I can even take their feelings and put them back into themselves, magnified, and then pull them back out into me, then send them *back* to them, magnified even more, over and over, in a split second, creating a loop that overloads their emotional circuits and pretty much fries the prefrontal cortex. I could have fried *your* prefrontal cortex, but instead, I decided to just absorb your feelings, and when I did, I saw someone who is *insanely* confused and *super* scared about the fact that he confronted a demon last night, but what I *can't* tell is if you're brave, or if you're stupid, so which one is it?"

Simon stared at her in open-mouthed amazement. "I thought empaths were a myth."

"Well that's funny, because I know you sought out a demon, and I don't know if you know how people work, but usually it's a lot easier for them to believe that there are people who feel other people's emotions on a deep and meaningful level than it is for them to believe that an all-powerful, supernatural, literal spawn of evil who lives in a wholly separate dimension that's dripping with fire and sulfur and the fury of a fallen god can just hop on over and show up in someone's attic. The only people who think an earthbound demon is more likely to exist than a human being with preternatural empathy are serial killers, because they don't *understand* empathy, and morons, so I guess I *do* have my answer about whether you're brave or whether you're stupid, because you don't look even *close* to smart enough to be a serial killer."

"I'm...smart," Simon said, clearly flustered. He waved his hands, trying to clear the air of the awkwardness that was weighing it down like lead. "And I'm not—I'm...listen, I'm plenty brave, okay?"

Abby pushed a button on the cash register, and the drawer popped open with a loud *DING*. Simon jumped and screamed. Abby stared at him over the top of her glasses.

"You can be brave and still be scared by loud noises!" Simon cried.

"Sure." Abby reached into the cash register and pulled out a set of keys. She closed the drawer. Then she put her hands on her hips and considered Simon. Finally, she said, "Either way, I think we should go for a ride."

Simon wrinkled his brow in confusion. "You and me?" he said.

"Yeah," Abby sighed.

"I just...wanted some tokens..." Simon explained, laying the ten-dollar bill on the counter.

"I know. And now you're going to get in my truck, and we're going to drive to East Templar."

Simon rubbed his forehead. He was losing a lot of ground in this conversation. "You have a truck?" he asked.

Abby ignored the question. She looked over at Virgil, who was rocking the busted token machine while cursing under his breath. She snapped her fingers to get his attention. "Hey. Rage Against the Token Machine. Are you with him?" she asked, indicating Simon with her thumb.

Virgil stopped assaulting the machine and frowned across the room. "Depends. What'd he do?"

"He tried to fight a demon," she called out.

"Hey, maybe we could talk about this a little more privately?" Simon said, nodding toward the children at the birthday party table. They had stopped their chattering and were staring at Abby.

But she shrugged them off. "Look, kids gotta know there are monsters out there. You think their parents are doing them any favors by pretending there wasn't a zombie in the graveyard this week?"

The birthday girl's eyes grew huge. She looked at her mother. "Mommy, are there zombies?" she asked.

"No," the mother said pointedly, staring daggers at Abby. "Come on, sweetie, time to go. This party is over." She started gathering up the protesting children.

"Zombies are real," Abby said loudly.

Simon placed his hand on her elbow, trying to guide her away from that side of the counter while the mother glared at them, her face turning dark red. "Hey, come on, give her a break...she'll tell her about monsters when she's ready," he whispered. "How did you know about the zombie?"

"Oh, yeah, I saw that, too," Abby said. "When you touched me. Hey, what happened to your sis—?"

"Wow, you really know how to clear a room," Virgil interrupted, clearly impressed, as he strode up to the counter. "By the way, your token machine's broken."

"More now than it was before," Abby said, rolling her eyes. She jangled the keys. "Come on. We're going for a ride."

Virgil shook his head. "It's not a great time. I need to play some Skee-Ball. I'm feeling really in the zone."

"Play later."

"I can't play later, I don't know if I'll be in the zone later. I'm in the zone now. I know you're new here, so you don't understand, but I've been racking up tickets at this Squeezy Cheez since sophomore year of high school. I have almost five thousand tickets, and I only need, like, three hundred more, and that Nerf gun is mine, and I *need* it."

"Fine," she said, coming out from behind the counter. "Stay here. We'll go."

"Well, I'm not going to stay here by *myself*," Virgil whined.

"Wait, *why* are we going to East Templar?" Simon said. His head was starting to ache, and he felt way behind in the conversation. "And I have my own car...I can drive myself."

Abby stopped. She screwed up her face and gave Simon a pained look. "Do you not care about using twice the amount of gas that we need to? Do you not *care* about global warming?"

"I think the environment is very important," Virgil offered.

"Great. Let's go." Abby knocked on the wall behind the counter, next to the doorway that led to the employees' back room. "I'm on break!" she called back to some unseen co-worker. It was met with a muffled, very bored-sounding reply. Abby grabbed a handful of Kit-Kat bars from wire rack against the wall, stuffed them into her jacket pockets, and headed toward the front door.

"Wait, stop...*why* are we going to *East Templar?*" Simon demanded, exasperated.

Abby turned around, walking backward, spinning the ring of keys on her finger. "We're going to meet a sorcerer," she said.

CHAPTER 10

"Can we talk about this 'sorcerer' thing for a second?" Simon asked, snatching desperately at the grab handle above the GMC's passenger window.

Abby threw the truck into a slide around a sharp curve and said, "Not now. I'm focusing on the road."

The four-door Sierra skidded around the corner, and Virgil, who wasn't wearing his seatbelt, went careening across the bench seat in the back. "Can I ask why we're riding in a car with a stranger?!" he asked, smacking the back of his head against the driver's side window. "I'm generally very trusting when it comes to strangers," he said, rubbing his head and flailing for his seat belt, "but this one is driving like a Bond villain, and I do *not* have health insurance!"

"You should be more responsible," Abby murmured. Her eyes were glued to the road ahead as she navigated the curves and bumpy cobblestone terrain of Old Templar, the original town settlement.

"Why aren't you taking the 85?" Simon asked, holding onto his handle for dear life.

"The 85 is murder at rush hour, and I only have an hour break."

They streaked around a corner that led into an alley, and the tailgate of the pickup skidded around and crashed into the broad side of a Dumpster. The two men inside the truck screamed. Abby gritted her teeth and pulled the Sierra back into her control as she roared down the narrow space between two buildings.

"This is an alley!" Virgil pointed out.

"It's a shortcut," Abby corrected him, gripping the wheel tightly.

They burst out into the street on the other side, and Abby slammed on the brakes, squealing the truck's tires around and lifting two of them up into the air as they pulled a ninety-degree turn. She gave the wheel a twist, and the tires slammed back down onto the asphalt. Then she sped away from the mess of cars that were screeching their tires and blaring their horns in their wake.

Eventually, she pulled them onto the ramp heading up to the interstate, and Simon took a breath. He let go of the grab handle and flexed the soreness from his hand. "Where are you taking us? Really? There hasn't been a sorcerer in Templar for...well, I don't know how long, but a long time. Decades, at least. Maybe centuries! My parents used to tell us stories about sorcerers that *their* parents had only heard of, so it's safe to say there hasn't been a sorcerer in Templar for a long time."

Abby shrugged. "There's one here now."

"And also, who are *you?*" Simon continued, ignoring her. "I don't even know why I got into this truck; I don't know you, and if you *are* in with a sorcerer, a *real* sorcerer, that's even worse! They're nothing but trouble, and that makes *you* trouble." He crossed his arms and sat back against the seat.

He knew it was stupid to get into a car with a stranger—especially a stranger who claimed to be taking him to a sorcerer, and *especially* one who drove like she drove. But there was something about her that he couldn't shake...something about her eyes, and her hair, and all the other things that he registered about her on some deep, subconscious level but really, *really* wished he didn't.

"Not all sorcerers are evil," she said sourly. "The fact that you would even say that is so *offensive*."

"She's right," Virgil said, popping over the back of the seat and pushing his face down in between theirs. "Some sorcerers are good. I mean, Merlin, for one."

"Merlin is a myth," Simon pointed out.

Abby scoffed. "You have to be joking."

"And for another," Virgil said, pushing on through their argument, "my cousin Rick told me he thinks one of his old neighbors from the LoDi district back when he was living there might have been a sorcerer, this old guy who kept bringing mason jars full of cloudy pink foams and things into his apartment."

"He was probably a serial killer," Simon said grumpily.

Virgil thought about that. "I guess he *could* have been a serial killer," he decided.

"If you want out, get out," was all Abby said as she sped along the interstate. The needle on the speedometer quivered near 90.

Simon frowned as he watched the pavement flash by outside his window. "Look, all I know about sorcerers is, they're incredibly powerful, and that much power almost always goes to your head, and most sorcerers turn evil."

Abby shrugged. "You haven't met this sorcerer," she said.

They drove along the interstate, looping over downtown Templar and cruising out toward the east, the sun still high in the western sky. Simon hadn't spent much time in East Templar; it was a transitional area between the rough parts of downtown and the bedraggled, economically depressed residential clusters in the Bypass Mountains, and it was dotted with old warehouses and trailer parks and industrial complexes with long-abandoned factories that had been left to rust several decades long past. "A sorcerer lives in *this* part of town?" Simon asked, glancing uncertainly out the window.

"What exactly do you think the going rate is for people who practice magic in a town where every single member of the population dedicates their entire lives to working hard to pretend like the supernatural doesn't exist?" Abby shot back.

Virgil tapped Simon on the shoulder. "She has a point," he said.

They drove on until they hit the River Road exit. Abby pulled off the interstate and slowed the truck as they approached the surface road that ran north along the dubiously named East River. The East River was really little more than a glorified drainage ditch—a wide, geometrical U-shaped concrete pour that served as the confluence for most of the storm drains that ran through Templar proper, flushed through with occasional overspills of water from the banks of the Raystown Branch of the Juniata River up north.

In other words, it was a huge concrete channel that ran through the eastern edge of Templar, and the liquid that trickled through was usually equal parts rainwater and waste.

Abby eased the truck over to the side of the road, near the Mallard Street Bridge, ramping the Sierra up onto the curb since there wasn't much of a shoulder to speak of. She turned off the ignition and popped open her door. "You guys ready?" she asked, dangling one leg out of the truck.

"Ready? Ready for *what?*" Simon asked, incredulous. "Three days ago, I didn't want anything to do with *any* of this! Then there's a zombie, and a demon—and *that* was terrifying—and now a *sorcerer?* No, I don't think I *am* ready!"

Abby shrugged. "Well, too bad. We're here." She jumped out of the truck and slammed the door behind her.

Virgil watched her go with awe. "She cares less about what you think than anyone I have ever known," he observed. A wide grin spread across his face. "I like her." He opened his door and leaped out after her.

"Great," Simon grumbled, fumbling with his seat belt and forcing open his door. "I'm the only one who's thinking straight."

He climbed out of the Sierra and followed them down into the concrete channel of Templar's East River.

CHAPTER 11

"The sorcerer lives beneath a bridge?"

Virgil screwed up his face in confusion as he stared at the tarps that had been draped over a series of exposed rebar jutting out from the concrete pylon beneath the bridge. An upturned shopping cart rested near the front flap, held in place on the concrete slope of the drainage ditch by two cinder blocks. A metal trash barrel was propped up on the other side of the tent, held even by a big wooden wedge that was similarly held in place with blocks. A few other cinder blocks were scattered across the concrete nearby. "Are we about to get mugged?" he asked Simon, careful not to let Abby hear.

"I'm starting to think we might be, yeah."

"So what if he lives under a bridge?" Abby asked with an edge of steel in her voice. She sounded defensive. "I *told* you he doesn't have money. Besides, he's not out here for him; he's out here for *you*. For all of us. He has powerful enemies...if they find him in Templar, they're going to come for him hard, and how many survivors do you think there'll be if a bunch of sorcerers go Super Saiyan in the heart of Midtown?" She pushed past them, annoyed. "You don't judge people by where they live," she murmured.

Simon blushed. "Sorry," he said quietly, staring down at his shoes.

"Sorry," echoed Virgil.

Abby marched up to the tarps. "Llewyn? I brought a couple of guys you should meet."

A pale hand emerged through the slit between the tarps. It pushed the canvas to one side, and out stepped a man, tall, broad, and old. He had long white hair that hung down in thick, twisted tendrils. He wore a wool, knee-length light blue coat with brass buttons, something a Union general might have worn during the Civil War. It bore the marks and stains of time. He wore a dirty white Henley shirt beneath it, and dark brown pants over a pair of scuffed leather boots. The skin on the sorcerer's hands and face was cracked and wrinkled, leathery in texture, but soft white, like the underbelly of a fish. A deep, pale scar crossed his lips from his left cheek down to the right side of his chin. He had one green eye, the rich, dark green of an Irish hillside after a rain shower. His other eyeball was missing; in its place, a bright blue light shone from the deep recesses of his eye socket, illuminating the hollow inside of his skull like a brilliantly-lit ice cave. The blue glow was so sharp, so piercing, that Simon had to shield his own eyes when the sorcerer stepped out of the tent.

"Llewyn the mage, meet Simon and Virgil, demon hunters," Abby said.

Simon and Virgil had never seen a human being as striking as this old man, and they had certainly never seen anyone with a burning blue light for an eye. They weren't sure how to react. Simon gave an awkward wave with one hand. Virgil actually bowed.

The old man grunted. "Small, for hunters," he said. His voice was rough and dry, as if he gargled with sand.

"And not very good at hunting, from what I can tell," Abby said, almost cheerfully. She pulled the truck keys from her pocket and gave them a twirl. "I have to get back. I'll leave you all to it." She turned and headed toward the truck.

Simon reached out and grabbed her elbow. "You're leaving us here?!" he asked, alarmed. She twitched at his touch, as his emotions seeped into her, but Simon wasn't thinking clearly enough to let go.

"Leave us all to what?" Virgil demanded.

Abby wrenched her arm free of Simon's grasp. "My break's almost over. You'll be fine."

"How are we supposed to get back?" Simon said, alarmed.

"Leave us all to *what?!*" Virgil asked again.

Abby stopped. She planted her hands on her hips. "You guys. Llewyn is a sorcerer who's here to battle the evil of Templar. You two are not-sorcerers who, for reasons I'm not entirely clear on, have also decided to battle the evil of Templar. You're a team now. I've made you a team. So go..." She twirled her hand in the air. "...*team.*" She turned and hiked back up the embankment toward the street. "I get off at ten," she called over her shoulder. "Come find me then." She reached the truck, pulled open the door, hopped into the driver's seat, fired up the engine, and tore away from the bridge, leaving Simon and Virgil behind with the sorcerer, their mouths hanging open in shock.

"Now what do we do?" Simon whispered.

Virgil shrugged. "I guess we...'team.'"

They turned back toward the sorcerer. A brilliant blue orb flashed toward them, crackling with energy. Simon cried out and tried to back out of the way, but he tripped over his own feet. He and Virgil collided. The streaking blue light split into two smaller balls. One slammed into Virgil, hitting him in the chest; the other exploded against Simon's shoulders. The energy balls burst with hard jolts that sent vibrating shocks through their whole bodies, and they collapsed in a heap onto the hard concrete of the drainage channel.

The wizard grunted. "Slow reflexes," he said.

"I thought we were a team," Virgil moaned, staring up at the blue sky.

"I need warriors. Not children," the wizard said gruffly. He stepped forward and lowered a hand. Simon looked at it warily, then reached out and grabbed hold. Llewyn pulled him to his feet. "Which are you?" the old man asked.

"I'm twenty-four years old, and he's twenty-five," Virgil said, indicating Simon as he pushed himself to his feet. "We're not children."

Simon nodded his agreement. "But...we're not warriors, either," he added.

The old man stared at them with his cold green eye. The blue light in his right socket pulsed twice, then dimmed to a dark, crystalline violet. "Honesty is a virtue among warriors," he said, giving them a satisfied nod. "Perhaps you can be taught." He stepped back toward his tent and pulled open the canvas flap. "Come in. We'll talk."

Simon and Virgil looked at each other uneasily. They had been friends long enough that they knew what each other was thinking without having to say it, and their consensus boiled down to this: *What are we going to do, try to run away from a sorcerer who shoots energy blasts?* They resigned themselves, Virgil with a shrug, and Simon with a sigh.

They stepped forward, ducked beneath the canvas, and stepped into the wizard's tent.

CHAPTER 12

"Don't touch anything. I forget what does what to which kind of people," Llewyn grunted.

Simon and Virgil stood just inside the entrance to the canvas tent. Their eyes were as big as saucers, and their jaws practically hung down to the floor. On the outside, the sorcerer's dwelling was a small, shabby, makeshift structure, just a few pieces of fabric thrown over bits of rebar. But on the inside, it was a massive, sprawling, luxurious mansion of unimaginable grandeur.

They found themselves in a stately foyer, with walls of dark, polished mahogany, and a floor of smoothly-hewn granite. The ceiling was built from enormous timbers, laid in a notched, cross-hatched fashion, with painted plaster frescoes adorning the squares between the beams. A large rug spread across the floor, a brilliant tapestry of reds, blues, oranges, and yellows. Torches set into iron bands in the walls flared with huge, bright flames, washing the foyer in light. The room opened up into a wider parlor with a double staircase, each set of stairs curving away from each other, then back again as they neared the mahogany landing of the second story. The floors in that farther room were white marble, and beyond the parlor, a wide hallway led into a darker area of the manor.

Simon stepped backward. He poked his head back outside. It was still a canvas tent, maybe ten feet in length. He stepped back inside. The mansion remained.

He found himself completely without words.

But, as usual, Virgil did not. "I'm sorry I thought you were definitely a crazy person and not an actual magician," he breathed, walking forward into the foyer and gazing up with wonder at the high ceilings. "I know I never said out loud that I thought you were a fraud, but I *did* think you were a fraud, even with the bright, shiny light thingy in your eye, which is a great effect, and it crossed my mind for a second that those energy blasts could have been just you shooting us with bottle rockets, 'cause I've done that before to people, and it's pretty funny, so I *did* think you were a fraud, and I want to be upfront about that, because we are in way, *way* over our heads, in a whole different league, and I want you to teach me everything you know about everything." His eyes traveled the length of the foyer ceiling and back down the wall, toward the door. They came to a rest on the sorcerer as he ducked his huge frame through the opening of the tent and joined them inside the room. "It also makes me think your eye is more than just a showpiece, and I am *very* excited and terrified to learn what *that's* all about."

"Things are rarely what they seem," was the sorcerer's simple reply. He pushed past the two young men and strode across the parlor, into the hallway on the far side. Simon and Virgil hurried to keep up with his long strides as they passed door after door set into the hallway. The sorcerer led them purposefully to the end of the hall, to a great wooden door that bowed out toward them, like a hubcap. He grasped the wrought iron handle and pulled the door open. "We'll speak more in here."

The chamber at the end of the hall was a perfect sphere, built from a series of carefully and artfully bent wooden planks. Simon had the distinct sensation of stepping inside a bocce ball as he crossed into the room.

A bridge-like platform extended into the center of the room, suspended over the curved floor of the chamber by two thick metal cables secured to the wall above the door. At the end of the platform was a stone basin set atop a marble pedestal. It looked like a tall fire pit, or a fountain. And it was the only object of interest in the room; the curved walls were smooth and bare, and though the spherical chamber was filled with a soft light, that light had no discernible source.

"I have so many questions," Virgil said, stepping into the room and following Simon onto the platform, looking around the chamber with awe. "I guess the most important one is, are we going to die in here?"

The sorcerer entered behind them and pulled the door closed. It shut with a heavy *CLUNK*. He turned to the other two men, his blue-light eye even more brilliant and crystalline in the softer light of the sphere. "If I wanted you dead, I'd have made a show of it outside," he said, and his mouth curled up into a smirk.

It was the first time they'd seen him smile. It sent shivers rippling down their spines.

He pushed past Simon and Virgil and stepped up to the stone basin. He placed his hands on the rim and leaned forward, staring down into the depths of the bowl. "My name is Llewyn Dughlasach," he said, and they noticed a soft Scottish lilt to his words. "I'm a kinesthetic mage of the Seventh Order. To answer what I assume are some of your questions: I am several hundred years old, old enough that I would have to work the sums to remember my exact age; my magic is True Magic, some of it inherited, most of it studied and learned; my dedicated purpose is to purge the world of evil, as far as I'm able; and no, I am not from Templar. I am from quite a different place." He drew himself up from the basin and turned to face his guests. He crossed his arms, and he gave a mighty exhale. "I'm guessing you have more questions. I'd like you to ask them now, if you would, so we can have them over with and turn our attention to more important matters."

Simon threw Virgil a look. Virgil returned it with a shrug.

"Okay," Simon said, clearing his throat. "I guess I have some questions. First of all, why are we here? And how do you know Abby?"

Llewyn nodded slowly. "Abby brought you here because she believes you can aid me in my quest. She came to Templar because she felt the pull of my call."

Virgil screwed up his face in confusion. "I don't know about anyone else, but I feel like a little bit of detail is going to go a *really* long way here."

Llewyn grunted. He wiped one huge hand down his face, and he looked tired...or maybe he just wasn't used to this much conversation. "As I said, my dedication is to purge the world of evil. I have long felt a powerful malignant energy emanating from this place. It reached me even in Europe, and now that I'm here, it stinks to me like a rotting animal." He wrinkled up his nose and shuffled with disdain and disgust. "There's a convergence of evil in this city, and it's growing stronger. More powerful. I imagine you feel it."

Simon nodded slowly. "Weird things have always happened here," he admitted. "Supernatural things that don't seem to happen anywhere else. And...yeah. They're happening more often."

"Your city of Templar sits above an intersection of preternatural energy fields that make it susceptible to ultra-dimensional invasion. That bad energy manifests sometimes as monsters, as demons, as who knows how many kinds of evil. But only on occasion. Only once every long while."

"Something has happened to bring the evil to life more often," Simon said, understanding as he spoke. "The intersection is becoming..." He searched for the right word. "...busier."

Llewyn nodded curtly. "Exactly right. Templar is in danger. *Serious* danger." The blue light in his right eye glowed even brighter, casting a glow against the wooden walls of the chamber. "I aim to stop it, if I can." He turned to the pedestal and placed his hands into the bowl. He closed his eyes, and though they were standing behind him, Virgil and Simon could see the soft and eerie glow of Llewyn's brilliant blue light glowing through the filter of his eyelid, illuminating the space in front of his brow like a halo.

The sorcerer began to mumble a spell; as he spoke, his hands began to glow orange, as if they held a secret fire. As he continued the incantation, the glow spread out from his hands and became a strange ball of thick light, almost as if formed from a semi-solid substance, like a gel. The outer rim was a vibrant, fiery orange, but the inside of the sphere–the core–was a grey-dappled black; they could see the darkness of it through the orange crust of the globe.

As the sphere became larger, filling the basin, the black edged out the orange, until the fiery color disappeared altogether, or maybe was sucked inside of it. Llewyn's lips stopped moving, and he opened his eyes, drawing his hands out of the stone bowl. He slipped his palms out of the sphere, shaking them free like he was pulling them from a vat of Jell-O, and the sphere closed up behind him, its asphalt gray coloring rushing in and filling the space left behind by his fingers. As they watched, the inside of the sphere began to churn; the orange bits collected in the swirl, forming into miniature balls of light. All of these balls met in the center of the sphere, and the whole globe spun so fast, it became a blur. Then, suddenly, it stopped, and the orange bits of light burst outward from the center, coming to quick, sharp stops in various spaces, spread throughout the inside of the globe. Some of them were the size of dimes; others were hardly more than specs of dust.

Llewyn beckoned the other two men forward. They glanced uneasily at each other, then cautiously approached the basin. "This is a map of Templar," the wizard said gruffly. Virgil opened his mouth to point out that it didn't *look* like a map, and Llewyn must have sensed what he was going to say, because he hurriedly added, "It's not a map *exactly*, but a spherical representation. See the orange areas?" The other men nodded. "Those are meta-power signatures. They measure the magical strength of different entities."

"There are *that* many magical beings in Templar?" Simon asked, startled. There were easily a few dozen orange spots on the map.

"It's surprising," the sorcerer agreed. He pointed to one of the larger orange spheres on the far side of the globe. "This one, here…that's Asag, the demon on Evergreen Street. The demon you two apparently decided to engage." He raised an eyebrow in Simon's general direction.

"It was his idea," Simon replied, pointing across the basin at Virgil.

Virgil scratched the back of his neck. "Templar needs heroes," he said uncomfortably, because he didn't know what else to say.

"Templar needs warriors who are trained in magic," Llewyn snapped. The gruffness of his voice was so powerful that Virgil shrank back, and for a second, Simon was worried he might accidentally step off the platform completely.

"We didn't know what it would be like," Simon admitted, bowing his head in embarrassment.

Llewyn shot him an annoyed look. "Obviously," he snarled. He turned his attention back to the globe. He pointed to another sizeable orange orb on the other side, across from the demon. "This is our location, here."

"Your energy isn't much bigger than the demon's," Virgil pointed out nervously. "Is that...bad?"

Simon expected an explosive reaction, but when Llewyn replied, his voice was calm. "Asag is an especially powerful arch-demon. He's ancient, with a long history of worship, and he holds a high rank in hell." The sorcerer sighed. "You would have had a hard time picking a worse demon to confront."

"He sort of made the decision for us," Virgil pointed out. "He came to us. We just...tried to do something about it."

"Try not to, until you've learned how to harness your energy," Llewyn said.

Simon cleared his throat uncomfortably. "Harness...*what* energy?" he asked. "We're not magic, we're not...we're not sorcerers, or witches, or anything."

"Warlocks," Virgil corrected him. "Guy witches are warlocks."

"We're not *magic*," Simon repeated. "I'm thinking it's probably best for us to just...not fight demons anymore."

Llewyn placed his hands on the globe and pulled them apart, and the section of the map with his light zoomed in and expanded. His power orb grew to the size of a fist, and Simon and Virgil could see two other dots, much smaller, but unmistakable, hovering near the larger energy signature. "See those?" the sorcerer asked. "Those two magic signatures, there?"

Simon furrowed his brow. "Who's that?" he asked.

Llewyn turned and looked at him gravely. "Those sources of magic are the two of you."

CHAPTER 13

"Those are *us?*" Simon asked, incredulous.

"They're not very big," Virgil pointed out with a frown.

"Why do they exist at all?" Simon demanded. "We don't have magic powers!"

"Oh, yeah, that's a good point," Virgil decided.

The sorcerer grunted. "Apparently you do."

Simon tilted his head, his face pinched in confusion. He backed away from the basin, raising his hands defensively, and moved along the platform toward the door. "Wait. I'm sorry, wait. Are you saying…are you saying that *we*—Virgil and I—are *magic?*"

"I'm saying you have no idea how to use it, and I can't even start to speculate how on earth it got there. But yes, you've got magic in you. Both of you."

Simon's knees turned to water under his own weight, and he fell down, collapsing on the walkway. "We're normal human beings," he said quietly, more to himself than to anyone else. "Normal humans don't have magical powers."

"They do if they've had it transferred into them—by a magical creature or a spell, or by a totem or a familiar. Some get the curse from spirits of the dead. Whatever the reason, you have power. Both of you."

"Whoa," Virgil said, his eyes wide. "This explains so much."

"It doesn't explain *anything*," Simon countered. His voice was shrill and tight. He scraped his hands through his hair, holding tight, trying to pull himself together.

"It explains why that candle protection spell worked," Virgil pointed out. "Even Asag said it was pretty good."

"You cast a protection spell?" Llewyn asked, his face brightening with curiosity.

"We lit a candle and said some words, and the demon couldn't get close while we held the candle," Virgil said proudly. Then he added, "Is that...good?"

"It's surprising," Llewyn said. "And it reinforces what we see here. You two have a gift."

Simon buried his face in his hands. He shook his head slowly, trying desperately to process all of this information. "This is just..." he started, trailing off into nothing. He sighed heavily, then tried again. "This is too much."

"It's amazing," Virgil countered. He hurried over to where Simon had crumpled on the walkway and crouched down to his level. "Dude! Seriously! Do you understand what this *means?*" He held out his hands, and he stared down at them in wonder, as if they were glowing with their own light and power, which they most certainly were not doing. "We are *actual heroes of Templar!*"

"You are inexperienced novices who have no idea how to manage their strengths," Llewyn interrupted. "But you have power. Abby felt that. That's why you're here."

"I'm sorry, Abby *felt* that?" Virgil asked, returning his attention to the sorcerer. "What does that mean?"

"She's an empath," Simon said.

"She's an extraordinarily powerful empath," Llewyn corrected him. He stabbed his finger against the globe, next to an orange light that was about the size of a pea. "This is Abby."

Virgil squeezed his eyes shut and shook his head. "I'm sorry, Abby is a *sorcerer?*" he cried.

"No!" Simon replied quickly, and passionately. Then he remembered that he actually didn't know much about her at all, and he drew back into himself. "I don't think so," he added quietly.

"She's not a sorcerer," Llewyn confirmed, sounding irritated. "She's an empath. Metaphysical powers manifest in different ways." He shot Virgil a look, and the light from his right eye burned darkly. "You're not a sorcerer either, in case you were wondering."

"I wasn't going to ask," Virgil lied.

"Abby is an empath, and her powers are unique. Extraordinary, really. She can't see your emotions unless she touches you, but she has an uncanny ability to sense feelings from an unheard of distance. And she has additional powers as well..." Llewyn's voice trailed off, and he suddenly looked troubled and lost in thought. After a few moments of silence, he shook his head to clear away whatever was troubling him. He blew on the globe, and the entire map disintegrated, the orange and asphalt-grey orb breaking into flakes and falling into the bottom of the basin. He turned and strode along the platform, toward the door. "Coming?" he asked over his shoulder.

Virgil gripped Simon at his elbows and pulled him to his feet. "Coming," he replied, and together, they stumbled along behind the sorcerer.

"The strength of your demon is startling. He needs to be stopped." Llewyn pushed through the door at the end of the walkway and passed out of the chamber. Virgil and Simon hurried after him. He led them back into the parlor, and he plopped down on one of the two floral-print sofas sitting on the plush rug. The springs groaned beneath his weight. "I felt him from half a world away."

Virgil led Simon to the other couch and lowered him onto it. He looked like he was in shock. Virgil sat down next to him, leaning forward with interest. "I don't want you to smite me or anything for asking personal questions, but since you bring it up—the part about you stopping him and everything—can I just ask, if your power signature is about the same size as the demon's, then...I mean...not to be disrespectful or anything, but why aren't *you* fighting him?"

Llewyn gritted his teeth so hard that Virgil could hear the squeak of it from across the room. The sorcerer's face darkened. "I'm inhibited," he said through a clenched jaw. He shrugged off his coat and gripped the hem of his shirt. He pulled it up to his neck, revealing a pale but well-defined stomach and a powerful chest. A solid streak of what appeared to be shiny, black stone bisected his breastplate, creating a lightning-bolt shape that started at his clavicle and ended just above his abdomen. He tapped the skin next to the streak, and it pushed in a bit, enough so that Simon and Virgil could see that his skin was wholly separate from whatever obsidian thing bisected his chest. Simon blenched.

"Don't you throw up," Virgil whispered, clapping a hand over Simon's mouth.

Llewyn didn't seem to hear him. He was too preoccupied with his own sadness, staring down forlornly at the black streak. "Two years ago, a dark mage named Morilan cast this into my chest. I had gone to the Carpathian Mountains to release the people there from the evil will of Morilan, and we struggled. Greatly. We were locked in battle for three days, and three nights. Near the end of it, we were both exhausted. I thought I would preserve my *mana* a bit by letting down my shield, only for a few moments." Llewyn's shoulders sagged, and his entire body tilted forward as he lowered his eyes in the defeat of the memory. "Morilan sensed it. He seized on it. With my shields down, he cast a dark blade, and it hit home." He traced his fingers thoughtfully over the external edge of the obsidian, lost deeply in thought. "The spell was meant to destroy me. It would have destroyed a lesser mage. But I refocused, I sent my strength into my chest, to hold the dark blade in place where it had sunk into my chest. It does not touch my heart, but only because I hold it at bay. If I were to let up on my focus, the blade would instantly slice through, wedge itself through a chamber of my heart, and I would die." He lowered his shirt, and he pulled his coat back over his shoulders, staving off a shiver. "I focus most of my energy now on this dark blade. It takes almost everything I have to hold it where it is. I'm not strong enough to remove it...I doubt the strength to do that exists on this plane. If I give up my fight for one instant, my life is over. What magic I have leftover, I use to the best of my abilities. I currently use a portion to provide a comfortable dwelling in a modest environment. I use a greater portion to send out a signal, here, from Templar, in an attempt to draw in other creatures of power, so that we might band together and defeat the extraordinary evil that is gathering here, in the dark recesses of the city. Your friend Abby answered the call. And now, you two have as well."

Llewyn reached forward and pulled the coffee table closer to his seat. Simon noticed for the first time that the table was actually a huge chest, with iron bands crossing the lid. The sorcerer placed his hand on the lock, and it fell open with a loud *CLUNK*. He pushed open the lid. Inside the trunk were hundreds of pouches and trinkets and fabric and jars, all cluttered together haphazardly. The sorcerer dug through the mess until he found the two pouches he was looking for. He pulled them out by their drawstrings and closed the lid. He tossed one navy blue pouch to Simon, and the other to Virgil.

Virgil caught his easily. Simon was still reeling from pretty much everything that had happened in the last 24 hours, and his pouch bounced off his chest and hit the floor. He snapped to attention and picked up the bag. It was light; whatever was inside weighed practically nothing at all. He pulled open the drawstring and shook the contents of the bag into his open palm.

Out tumbled a thick, metal wrist cuff. It appeared to be old, and made of iron, at least two inches wide, and a quarter-inch thick. It looked like it should have had some heft to it, but it felt as light as a feather in his palm. A hinge bisected the cuff, allowing it to break open so a person could secure it around his wrist and close it up again.

"I don't wear bracelets," Virgil said, frowning down at the cuff in his hand. It looked like Simon's, except instead of a dark gray metal, his was a lighter color, almost the color of ivory, but it, too, appeared to be made of a heavy, solid metal. "Not really into the whole jewelry thing."

"They're not bracelets. They're manacles."

Virgil looked doubtfully at the bracelet. "I'm not really into manacles, either…"

"Not manacle, *mana*-cle. Emphasis on 'mana.'" He closed the trunk and stood up from the couch. "Follow me."

The sorcerer strode toward the entrance to the tent. Simon looked at Virgil. Virgil shrugged. He hefted the cuff a few times, as if to see if the lightness of it was real, then he followed Llewyn out of the room. Simon followed.

"You have mana," the sorcerer said, reaching into the trash barrel and pulling out an empty tin can. "Both of you. You haven't realized it because the energy is weak. And the energy is weak because you haven't been taught how to harness it. The energy is too weak to present itself naturally." He set the tin can on top of the overturned shopping cart, balancing it on the metal grating. "It's more common than you think. Lots of people are either born with magic in their blood, or they have it transferred upon them, but they never think to look for it." He turned back to the two young men, and the blue light of his missing eye gleamed with mischief. "Let's see what happens when we look for yours."

Virgil perked up at that. "We're going to actually *do* magic?" he asked.

Llewyn shrugged. "We'll see." He nodded at Virgil's cuff. "The manacle goes on the wrist of your non-dominant hand."

"Isn't your dominant hand stronger?" Simon asked, though he pulled open the cuff and clasped it over his left wrist anyway.

"Strong enough that you use it without thinking. The non-dominant hand takes more focus. You'll need that focus to channel your energy."

Virgil closed his cuff around his right wrist. He held up his arm in the dying sunlight and flexed his fingers. "Feels like magic," he decided.

"I don't feel anything," Simon frowned.

"That's what magic feels like," Virgil replied.

"Quiet," the sorcerer chided.

Both men looked down at their feet, embarrassed. "Sorry," they murmured in unison.

Llewyn crossed back over to the tent and stood next to them, facing the cart and the can. "The manacle acts as a harness. Strictly speaking, you don't need the manacle to manifest your energy, but it will help you control the power. Without the manacle, you run a great risk of causing injury and death, to others and to yourself. Understood?"

Both young men nodded.

"The manacle will collect your magic, store it, and hold it until you decide to release it." He pushed up his left sleeve and revealed a manacle of his own, a solid circle of dull black metal. He closed his hand into a fist, and the cuff began to glow a deep orange. Tiny streaks of light flowed toward the cuff through the sorcerer's body, flicking beneath his skin like embers and collecting in the metal of the cuff, which grew brighter and brighter as more grains of magic flooded down his arm. He turned, reached toward one of the cinder blocks, and opened his hand. Three concentric rings of orange light exploded out from the cuff, encircling his wrist. They rotated lazily, each spinning oppositely of the next, and the space between the rings was filled with ancient runes, written in orange as if they had been stamped in the air with fire. Then the rings pushed themselves outward, moving past his hand and lining themselves up in order from largest to smallest so that they looked like a mystical telescope in reverse. Then Llewyn's palm began to glow with a hot orange ball of light, and when he flicked his fingers, the light burst forward, rocketing through the tunnel of orange rings and screeching toward the cinder block. It exploded on impact, blowing the concrete brick to dust.

"Whoa!" Virgil cried, jumping behind Simon for cover. "That was *awesome!*"

"We can do *that?*" Simon breathed, his mouth open in awe. He stared down at the cuff on his own wrist, incredulous.

"Not yet," Llewyn said gruffly. "But maybe someday, with the right training."

"I want to try," Virgil decided, his voice firm and definite. He stepped out from behind Simon and rubbed his hands together. "I want to blow up a brick."

"We'll see how you fare with the can," Llewyn smirked.

Virgil held up his wrist, inspecting the cuff. "How does it work?" he asked.

"Make yourself mindful of your energy," the sorcerer instructed, crossing his arms and assuming the role of teacher. "Feel your depths. Find your *mana*."

Virgil frowned. "I...don't know how to do that."

Llewyn sighed. He tried again. "Close your eyes." Virgil did. "Imagine a ball of energy in the pit of your stomach. Imagine you can feel its warmth. Take your happy memories, and your friendships, and your family, put them all into that ball. Can you feel it?"

Virgil concentrated. He pictured a ball of bright light glowing in his stomach. He didn't know how to put happy memories into a place, so instead of trying, he just let them sort of wash over him. Keeping the ball of light in his mind, he thought back to the time when his dad had taken him to Kings Island for his twelfth birthday...and the time that Suzie Grafton had kissed him next to the bleachers in high school...and the times he and Simon had gone camping on Camelback Mountain, when they had spent the evenings roasting hot dogs and marshmallows, and telling ridiculous ghost stories. Virgil smiled, and the ball of light in his stomach grew brighter in his mind, and warmer.

He actually *felt* its warmth.

"I do feel it," he whispered, barely moving his lips. He was afraid if he moved too much, he would disturb the light, and it would evaporate.

"Good," Llewyn nodded. "Now push it up. Let it melt into your bloodstream. Carry the energy through your entire body."

With his eyes still closed, Virgil pictured the ball of light flattening and spreading, coating the inside of his body like a brilliant paint. He began to actually feel the warmth of the light tingle against his skin.

"Virgil," Simon whispered, his voice quiet with awe. "Look."

Virgil opened his eyes. It wasn't just his imagination; his skin actually was lit up from the inside. His blood glowed with brilliant yellow-orange color, streaking through his veins and giving his skin a warm glow. As he watched, the light flowed toward his right wrist. He saw it drain from the fingers of his left hand and disappear up his arm, and he could feel the heat flushing across his shoulders and down into his right arm. The metal cuff began to draw the energy into itself, soaking in the orange light and glowing as brightly as fire. The color slipped from his skin fully into the manacle. He held up his wrist and gazed at the bright orange metal in awe. It was warm on his wrist, but not hot enough to burn. "I'm a sorcerer," he breathed.

Llewyn snorted. "Not even close."

Virgil inspected the glowing cuff carefully. He reached out with his other hand and touched it. The tip of his finger tingled, but it didn't burn. "How do I shoot it?" he asked, mesmerized.

"Aim your wrist at the can," the old man instructed. "The manacle is the chamber; your hand is the muzzle. Got it?" Virgil nodded. "Good. When you're ready, focus all your concentration on the energy in the cuff. You'll feel it build."

"I feel it building," Virgil confirmed, concentrating so hard that beads of sweat began to form on his forehead. And indeed, the cuff began to glow with even more intensity.

"Good," Llewyn nodded. "Keep going. When it builds so much you don't feel like you can contain it anymore, you push it out."

"Push it out how?" Virgil asked. His hand was beginning to shake.

"Push it out from your gut. It's like breathing out, hard."

The manacle was so saturated with energy that the metal now appeared to be made of molten steel. It was actually humming with power; Simon could hear it, even standing six feet away. The power of it sent Virgil's arm into tremors, and he struggled to keep his aim steady. "Okay," he said through clenched teeth, "here I go."

He squeezed his eyes shut, and he clenched the muscles in his stomach. He took a deep breath, and as he exhaled, he threw his whole self into the manacle, and the energy exploded out from the cuff.

There was a quick flash with a loud *POP!* as a halo of light burst out from the manacle. Then a small explosion, like a bottle rocket popping, burst in the air just above his hand. Finally, a bundle of orange light the size of a softball shot out from his knuckles. It zoomed forward, missed the tin can by ten feet, shot into the embankment, ricocheted off, slammed into the concrete on the other side of the ditch, and bounced again, shooting straight up into the air, rising higher and higher until it disappeared into the night sky, a falling star in reverse.

All three men watched quietly as the ball of light faded into space. It disappeared just to the left of the blinking lights of an airplane, cruising high above in the sunset sky.

"Well," Simon said, clearing his throat. "*That's* going to be on the news."

"Next time, try not to miss so hard," Llewyn grumbled. He nodded at Simon. "You're up."

Simon swallowed, hard. He took a few deep breaths to steady his nerves. "Okay," he said. He stepped forward and lifted his left arm.

"You know what to do?" the sorcerer asked.

Simon nodded. He closed his eyes and thought back on happy thoughts. He was surprised at just how few and far between they were. But before long, he had collected a small set of them: autumn afternoons of his childhood, crunching through the hills of southern Pennsylvania with Virgil; rainy Saturday movie marathons with his mom; the bonfires during Homecoming, when he felt shrouded in night, and somehow both separate and together with the other people in his class; the way Abby smelled, like peppermint and gingerbread; his sister, Laura, driving him to the riverfront so they could watch the fireworks on the Fourth of July, singing along with the radio and laughing.

He opened his eyes. His manacle was ablaze with energy and light, glowing with a powerful aura the emanated from the metal.

"Good," Llewyn said, sounding pleased. "That is very good."

Unlike Virgil, Simon's hand didn't shake. His wrist didn't feel taxed at all. In fact, it felt comfortable. It felt *right*. It felt like his arm had been missing the magic of the manacle his entire life, and was only just now becoming a whole appendage.

He pointed his open hand at the can. He felt a sense of calm wash over him, and the world came into a crisp focus, as if every single thing in sight was outlined in heavy black ink. He homed in on the can, and it seemed to grow larger as he focused. He felt the fire in his stomach, and he pushed it up, pushed it out, through his shoulder and down his arm. The energy in the manacle gathered itself and grew so bright that it was almost a second sun. He gave one more push, and the energy shot forward...but just as it did, he had a vision, a crystal-clear view of Mrs. Grunberg's dark basement, of the demon sitting in his chair, with the porcelain baby mask squeezed tightly onto his face. It was like the demon was looking at him, was *seeing* him, even though he was on the other side of town. And then, in the vision, Asag said his name: "*Simon*."

It all happened in a flash. Simon flinched, surprised by the dark vision, just as the energy burst out of his cuff. The ball of light went wide, slamming into the broad side of the shopping cart and melting the metal wire grate.

"Close," Llewyn said, sounding impressed. He raised an eyebrow and stared at Simon with his one green eye. The blue light in the other eye socket dimmed into its dark crystalline violet. "Is everything okay?"

"Yeah," Simon lied. "Just—yeah. Fine."

He could still see the afterimage of Asag burned into his vision.

CHAPTER 14

"I can't keep the manacle?" Virgil asked, disappointed.

Llewyn grunted. "The manacles stay with me. When you earn them, you can keep them."

"How long before we earn them?"

Llewyn thought about this, rubbing the thick stubble along his chin. "Three years, I think," he said finally.

"Oh, come on," Virgil complained.

Llewyn held open the pouch. Virgil sighed and dropped his manacle into it. Simon slipped his cuff into his pouch as well and handed it over to the sorcerer. "You've got talent," the old man admitted, cinching the bags and tossing them into the trunk. "Both of you. But we've got a lot of work to do." He closed the lid and turned to face the young men. He crossed his great arms, striking an incredibly imposing figure. "Come back tomorrow morning. Eight o'clock. We'll train more then."

"Eight?" Virgil asked. "I can't, I have a job."

"Quit your job," Llewyn said simply.

Virgil laughed. "I can't quit my job, I *need* my job."

"He does need his job," Simon confirmed. "Or else he can't pay rent. I really need him to pay his half of the rent."

"What about you?" Llewyn asked, turning toward Simon. "Do you have a job?"

"Sort of," Simon said. "I walk dogs."

"Simon doesn't need a real job," Virgil added, rolling his eyes like he always did when he talked about Simon's financial situation. "He walks dogs because he gets bored just sitting at home. His grandpa invented the drive-thru window, and now he's set for life."

Llewyn looked at Simon, surprised. "Is that true?" he asked. Simon nodded, blushing with embarrassment. But Llewyn nodded seriously. "That is a good invention," he said.

"Yeah, well, all *my* grandpa invented was bad jokes that were super racist," Virgil said sourly. "So I have to work. I can come after."

"Come at eight," the sorcerer insisted. "Fighting evil is your job now."

"That is a very cool job description," Virgil admitted. "And it's not like I love working at the plant. But I need that job. I'm barely paying my bills as it is."

"It's true," Simon confirmed. "He's not very good with money."

"Fighting evil is your job now," Llewyn repeated. He reached into the pocket of his blue coat and pulled out a worn leather wallet. He tossed it to Virgil, who caught it against his chest.

"What's this?" he asked.

"It will fill with paper money for any expense that I deem reasonable," the sorcerer said. "It's payment for your training."

Virgil stared at the wallet in disbelief. "Seriously?" he said. Llewyn nodded.

"Holy Hamburg, I *love* fighting evil," he marveled.

"Do you require one as well?" Llewyn asked Simon.

Simon shook his head. "No, that's okay," he said. "I'm good."

The sorcerer nodded. "Come back at eight," he said. "Come ready to focus. Asag's power grows, and if he isn't stopped, he may soon plunge all of Templar into darkness."

Simon sighed. "Do you really think we're the best people for the job?" he asked.

Llewyn shrugged. "You're the *only* people for the job," he said gruffly. "I'll keep sending out a beacon, try to draw others to our aide. Until then, you are the heroes of Templar."

Simon and Virgil looked at each other. Virgil smiled. Simon frowned.

"Until tomorrow," Llewyn said. He raised one hand and turned it in a wide circular movement. The air began to ripple and swirl, like water being spun down a drain. Then it turned color and became a dark purplish circle as the sorcerer opened up a portal to another part of town. Through the portal, Simon could see the flashing neon lights of the Pop-A-Shot and Whack-A-Mole games in the Squeezy Cheez.

"So we just...step through?" Simon asked uncomfortably.

Llewyn nodded. "That's how portals work."

Virgil tapped the leather wallet against his palm as he walked into the portal. "See you tomorrow," he said happily, and he popped through the circle, stepping into the Squeezy Cheez on the other side.

Simon nodded. "Tomorrow," he said. Then he followed his friend through the portal.

The sorcerer looked after them for a few seconds, his face marked with a grave and worried expression. Then he waved his hand, and the portal closed, severing the tie between them.

CHAPTER 15

"So? How did it go?" Abby asked. She held a spray bottle in one hand and an old, stained rag in the other. She misted the countertop and gave it a half-hearted swipe with the rag. But her eyes were alive with a brilliant light behind her oversized glasses.

"It was...weird," Simon decided.

"Definitely weird," Virgil confirmed.

"We shot magic from our hands."

"We did shoot magic from our hands."

"Virgil almost hit a plane," Simon said.

"I'm going to be on the news," Virgil smiled proudly.

Abby's eyes grew wide with interest. "*You two* have actual *magic?*" she asked.

Simon frowned. "You don't have to sound so surprised about it," he said, sounding hurt.

"It's just, you know magic is rare, right?" Abby continued wiping at the counter. "I know it seems sort of normal, because Templar is some weird evil-spirit hellstorm, but in *most* of the country, in most of the *world*, magic is super rare. The fact that you two have it is..." She shrugged. "Well, yeah, it's sort of surprising."

"You have magic, too," Virgil pointed out. He was only half-listening to the conversation. His attention was being drawn away by the bright lights of the Skee-Ball machines along the far wall. He was, for the hundredth time, trying to calculate how many more points he would need to score total to get enough tickets to finally, *finally* get the Nerf gun.

"I know *I* have magic. It's just surprising that *you* have magic."

"I feel insulted," Virgil said, not sounding one bit insulted. "Do I have time for a game?" He started walking toward the Skee-Ball machines.

"No," Abby said, "We're closed." She moved to the computer and tapped on the screen a few times. The bank of dim ceiling lights above the Skee-Ball games went completely out, snuffing that side of the room into total darkness, except for the ever-flashing neon lights from the games.

"Aw, come on," Virgil grumbled.

"Sorry, pal," Abby shrugged. "Time and Squeezy Cheez wait for no one." She put away the spray bottle and rag, and she gathered the trash bag out of the can next to the counter. "Besides, we have somewhere to be."

Simon started. "We do?" he asked. "I sort of thought we'd all go home and...maybe just sort of...process." He indicated the entire world with a sweeping motion of his hand. "Process everything."

"No time to process," Abby said, shaking her head. "We've got work to do."

"*More* work?" Virgil groaned. But the groaning was just for show. Energy-shooting magic-hero work was a lot more fun than what most people traditionally thought of as "work."

"What sort of work?" Simon asked cautiously.

Abby hauled the trash bags toward the back door, stopping to peek her head inside the back room and tell whatever manager was back there that she was clocking out for the night. "Come on," she called to the guys, and they trotted after her, toward the back exit. "We'll dump the trash, then I'll follow you over."

"Follow us over where?" Simon asked.

"To the old lady's house," Abby said, shoving open the door with her hip and stepping out into the alley. "I want to see this demon."

CHAPTER 16

"Is this a good idea?"

Simon was hunched nervously over the steering wheel of the old Pontiac. His eyes darted between the dark road ahead and the rearview mirror above, where he kept a close watch on the headlights of Abby's truck behind him.

"No. It is very obviously not a good idea," Virgil said, as if this were the stupidest question he'd ever heard. "I don't know if you remember, but last time we confronted the demon, he teleported me out of the house and showed you his face that was apparently so ugly it made you black out."

Simon remembered the flash of the demon that he had seen during the training session with Llewyn just an hour earlier. He shuddered. "We're not confronting the demon," Simon said, his voice resolute. "We'll show her the house, from a safe distance, she'll see the red light, and we'll go."

"Yeah," Virgil said, nodding enthusiastically, "Abby *definitely* seems like the kind of person to just sit back and do whatever you tell her to do."

Simon sighed. "Yeah," he said, shaking his head. "I don't feel good about it, either."

His hands were sweaty against the vinyl covering of the steering wheel, and he wiped his palms on his shirt, one after the other, so he could get a better grip.

"So, hey...did you catch what Llewyn said? About Abby?" Virgil asked. He watched Simon's face closely for his reaction.

"About her magic?" Simon replied.

"Yeah."

Simon nodded. "Yes. I caught that."

"He sounded kind of weird about it, right? I mean, that's not just me...is it?"

"No," Simon confirmed. "It's not just you." He raised his eyes to the rear view mirror again. Abby's headlights were close on his tail. "It sure sounded like she might be more than just an empath."

"And he also sounded kind of scared of her, didn't he?"

"I don't know," Simon admitted. "But yeah. It sort of sounded like maybe he was."

They drove on in silence for a while, navigating the crowded streets of Templar, heading west. When they were just a few blocks from Mrs. Grunberg's house, Virgil cleared his throat and said, "So you like her, right?"

Simon's cheeks burned. But he knew there was no sense lying to Virgil. His best friend knew his own thoughts almost as well as he did. In some ways, they were practically the same person. "Yeah," he said. "I like her."

Virgil nodded. "Thought so," he said. He sat back in his seat and lost himself quietly in thought. Eventually, he added, "She might have enough magic to literally rip you in half."

"Yes, Virgil, thank you, I understand that," Simon said, irritated.

Virgil nodded thoughtfully again. "Just making sure," he said.

"Thanks."

He turned onto Evergreen Street and pulled the car into an open spot at the side of the road, a block and a half south of Mrs. Grunberg's house. Abby pulled her truck in a few spaces down.

"Okay," Simon said, exhaling as he turned off the ignition. "We stay on this side of the street, we show her the house, and then we go," he said.

"Sure," Virgil agreed. "Sounds good to me."

"Okay."

He popped open his door. Abby was already walking up to the Pontiac. "Is *that* the house?" she asked, pointing up the road toward Mrs. Grunberg's house. "It is, isn't it? I could feel it half a mile away." Simon opened his mouth to speak, but Abby didn't wait; she checked for traffic, then jogged off across the road, heading toward the sidewalk on the other side.

"Well, this is going well," Virgil observed.

"Shut up," Simon muttered.

The guys followed her across the street. Abby came to a stop at the corner. Even though it wasn't far, Simon and Virgil were both breathing hard by the time they reached her. "If you two are going to fight evil, you might want to hit the treadmill every once in a while," she said, but not unkindly. She walked briskly toward the house.

"We should probably keep a good distance," Simon said.

"Yeah, seriously, Abby—that demon's no joke," Virgil added, hurrying to keep up.

"You guys, it's fine. I'm not going to try to go *into* the house," Abby said, rolling her eyes. "I'm not going to go poke the demon. I just want to get closer, and it's going to be fine. How many people are walking past it every hour, with no clue it's there? Dozens? Hundreds?"

Simon had to admit, she had a point.

"It's going to be fine," she repeated.

"We should have brought a bat or something," Virgil muttered.

"I really don't think a bat would do much against Asag," Simon said.

"Asag's not the one I'm worried that we might have to knock out," Virgil replied.

Simon looked up after Abby. "Oh."

She reached the edge of Mrs. Grunberg's property and crouched behind the end of the fence that separated the old woman's yard from the apartment building next door. The guys crouched next to her, with Virgil peering over their shoulders to try to get a good look at the house. "Is it still there?" he whispered.

"Yeah," Simon said, swallowing hard. "It's still there."

The pulsing red heartbeat glow filled the basement windows, getting brighter, then dimmer; brighter, then dimmer. And maybe Simon's mind was playing tricks on him, but this time, it seemed like every time the lights got brighter, the house actually expanded, the walls bowing outward and then contracting again when the light dimmed. As if the house was breathing.

The begonias were covered even more thickly in the liquid black shadow. The wet darkness dripped more quickly, and more frequently, creating smoking shadow puddles on the walkway.

"Well, that's not normal," Abby said, taking in the scene.

"Right. So can we go?" Simon asked nervously.

"Hold on. I want to get closer."

Before they could protest, Abby was off again, crouching low to the ground and running into the front yard. She jogged up behind the oak tree near the corner of the house.

"Hey, look...some of our salt is still there," Virgil said, pointing down at the wet, broken line of salt crystals in the grass.

"You guys made a salt ring?" Abby asked. She nodded her approval. "Nice."

Simon's chest grew warmer, and his toes began to tingle. "Thanks," he said bashfully.

But Abby held a finger up to her lips. She had just noticed something. She inclined her head, leaning in and trying to hear it more clearly. Simon held his breath and listened, too.

And then he heard it.

The house actually *was* breathing.

As the lights got brighter, and the walls swelled outward, and the house inhaled; when the lights got dimmer, and the walls pulled back inward, and the house exhaled. It was a low, rumbling sort of breath that vibrated the very grass they stood on.

"You didn't tell me the house could breathe," Abby said.

"It was *not* doing that before," Virgil said. "The lights, yes; the breathing, no."

"And it wasn't expanding, either," Simon said.

Abby nodded thoughtfully. "Asag's power is growing," she said. "We should tell Llewyn. We're running out of time."

"Time for what?"

"Time to defeat Asag. Whatever he's planning, he needs to build up enough strength to do it. Based on the house, I'd say he's getting close." She pointed at the wet, black begonias. "See that? That's called *umbrasis*. Asag is turning the flowers into living shadows. That's a sign of advanced strength."

"They were like that last night, too," Simon said quietly. "Not as bad as it is now, but...yeah."

Abby gritted her teeth. "Asag has to be put down."

"Okay, yes, sure. But...not tonight," Simon said nervously. "Right?"

"Sure...right..." Abby said. But she sounded distracted. She sank to her knees and shook out her hands. She placed one hand on the ground in front of her, pressing her palm into the grass.

"What're you doing?" Virgil whispered.

"Shh," she whispered back. "Concentrating."

Virgil and Simon crouched uncomfortably behind her, watching the house expand and contract. Abby knelt as still as stone, except for her own breath, which slowed over the course of a minute so that her breaths matched the house's breaths perfectly.

The blades of grass near her fingers began to tremble. Simon gasped as they bent toward her, as if the grass itself was bowing to Abby's hand. The ring of affected grass widened, and more and more of the blades in the yard bent over, leaning in toward Abby. The circle expanded and expanded, until all the grass between the tree and the house was hunched over, pointing toward their hiding spot.

"Simon," Virgil whispered. "Look."

The lights from the basement were growing darker. They were still fluctuating with the house's breath, but the brightness wasn't so bright anymore, and the dimness was practically solid darkness. As they watched, and as Abby breathed, and as the blades of grass bent toward them, the demon's light got fainter and fainter. Soon, it had fallen to nothing more than a steady, dark-red burn, like the glow of a shuttered furnace.

Simon felt something in his stomach clench. "Abby...what are you doing?"

But she didn't respond. Her eyes were closed, and her lips were moving, murmuring something in a secret language.

Simon felt something strange in the tips of his fingers. They prickled with numbness, and the sensation moved quickly across his palms and up his arms. His legs grew weak, and he fell onto his knees. Abby was too preoccupied to notice, and Virgil didn't sense anything wrong.

The cold, numb tremble crept across Simon's whole body, filling his chest so he could no longer feel his heart hammering. He tried to cry out, but his vocal chords were numb, too, and he couldn't make a sound. The pins-and-needles feeling moved up his skull, tingling at his eyes. As the sensation covered his face, a static blackness blanketed his vision, falling over it like a bad television signal. He sank down in the grass, screaming inside, seeing nothing and making no sound.

But then, through the darkness of his vision, a red light began to glow—the light from inside the basement. It didn't get brighter or dimmer; it just grew wider, spreading across the darkness, changing the fuzzy blackness into vivid red, until it was all he could see. Then a figure began to melt forth from the blood-red field. It resolved itself into a shape of the huge, hulking demon in a finely-tailored suit, his face covered with a white porcelain baby mask. "Simon," the demon whispered, growing larger in his vision, expanding against the red light. "Siiiimooonnnnn…" The demon lifted a hand to his mask and pushed it up. The shadow of the porcelain fell across Asag's face, and Simon's heart began to hammer in his chest as the shadow lifted, and he saw the demon's true visage.

"*Simon!*"

Simon snapped back to himself. He blinked; his vision cleared instantly. Asag vanished, and the red light was replaced by the sight of Mrs. Grunberg's yard. Virgil was standing over him, his hands on Simon's shoulders, shaking him. "Hey. Are you okay?"

Simon blinked. He gave his head a good shake, to clear the confusion. "Yeah," he lied. "I'm good."

Abby's attention was still focused on the house, and the light coming from the basement windows. "We should probably keep it down," she said, sounding distracted. "It's probably weird enough for people walking by that we're hiding behind a tree in an old lady's yard."

As if on cue, a new voice materialized from behind them: "What are you doing hiding behind a tree in my grandma's yard?"

All three of them jumped. They spun around to see a young man standing behind them, a brown paper bag cradled tightly in his arms. He was younger than them, but not by much, probably just out of high school. He had bright orange hair and pale, white skin, covered with freckles. His large brown eyes had dark circles beneath them, and he looked like he hadn't slept in weeks. His shoulders sagged, and his eyelids drooped. Simon was exhausted just looking at him.

"What are you doing here?" he demanded again. The paper bag looked heavy; he shifted it from one arm to the other, frowning down tiredly at the three strangers crouched in the grass.

"Oh. I...um. I..." Virgil stammered. "I...dropped my...con...tact?"

"He dropped his contact," Abby quickly confirmed, taking control of the conversation with remarkable confidence. "It's his last pair. Would you help us look?"

The young man squirmed uncomfortably. He obviously did not want to help them look. "I...need to get inside," he said, his voice weighed down with exhaustion. He skirted around them, keeping his eyes trained on them as he moved toward the front porch. "But you guys shouldn't be here."

"Why not?" Virgil asked. "Got something hidden in the basement?"

Simon elbowed him in the ribs. He groaned in pain.

"Private property," the young man murmured. "Just...you should go." Then he turned and climbed the stairs, fumbled with his keys, and disappeared into the house.

Abby looked at the Simon and Virgil. "Well, that was weird," she decided.

Simon pushed himself up to his feet and brushed off his knees. "Come on. Let's get out of here," he said.

But Abby looked directly into his eyes, holding him with her stare. "What did you see?" she asked.

"Nothing," Simon said. "I didn't see anything. Let's go."

Abby hesitated. She seemed to be working something out in her mind. "Simon...I'm not going to touch you. I'm not going to empathize. I could do that. But I won't. Because I think we need each other. All three of us. I think we're in this together, and we have to trust each other." Her blue eyes blazed. "But I need to be able to trust you. We all need to be able to trust each other."

Simon tried to hold her gaze, but he found himself completely unable to do so. He looked away, staring down into the grass. "If I saw something that I thought I should tell you about, I would tell you about it," he said. It wasn't a lie, exactly.

Abby bit at her lower lip, considering him closely.

Virgil leaned in, breaking the air between them. "Sorry, am I missing something? Are you...seeing things? Things that aren't a house and a light and a demon and some nerd with groceries?"

"No," Simon said, brushing past Virgil and heading back toward the Pontiac. "Come on, we need to go."

"I always, always, always hate to say this, but I think Simon's right." Virgil shuddered. "That kid weirded me out."

"That kid hasn't slept in days," Abby replied, her voice thick with concern. "He has an extraordinarily powerful hellspawn camped out in his basement. You wouldn't imagine the strength of the negative vibe that sort of presence radiates."

"I might," Virgil frowned. He looked on as Simon trudged back toward the street. "Simon might, too."

Abby looked over her shoulder, considering the old house. Lights—regular, everyday yellow-white lights—flicked on as Mrs. Grunberg's grandson moved through the house. There was another light on in the top floor, a dim light, as if from a lamp. It was likely Mrs. Grunberg's bedroom.

"Look," Abby said, nodding up at the house. "Look at those lights. This is a *home*. At least, it's *meant* to be a home. But a demon moves into the basement, cloaks himself from the inhabitants, so they have no idea that he's down there...just sitting there, in the darkness, draining their power, soaking in their strength. He's killing them. Slowly, and painfully. He's killing them." She crossed her arms and stabbed at the earth with the toe of her shoe. Then she added in a whisper, "You can't possible know how that feels."

"My mutant power is not empathy," Virgil admitted. When he heard his own words, his eyes grew large, and his face flushed pale. "Not that you're a mutant," he added quickly.

Abby nodded and waved him off. "It's okay," she said, smiling. "I know what you mean."

Virgil fidgeted awkwardly. "Well..." he said, trailing off as he looked up the street. Simon had made it back to the car, and he was leaning on the hood, shooting impatient looks back at Virgil. Virgil nodded at him. "We're definitely going to help them," he said, turning back to Abby. "That's what we're doing. Right? That was our plan all along. I mean, man, that's why we broke in and *faced the demon*. And now we have a real wizard teaching us how to take it down! We're going to help them, Abby. Definitely. That's the whole plan. I mean, it's the only plan, really," he shrugged. He looked doubtfully down at the deep red glow rising and falling through the basement windows. "It's just...now's probably not right. You know?"

Abby sighed. She nodded. "Yeah," she said. "I know."

"I mean, we thought we were ready, and we weren't. We were *not*. The monster just blinked, and I was teleported from in there to over there," he said, jerking his thumb at the spot where he'd come back to consciousness. "And Simon...I don't know what happened to Simon, but *something* happened, and he won't tell me what, but he has not been the same since."

Abby frowned. "So he's not always that...I don't know... odd?"

"Well. He's always odd. Just not *so* odd."

"Hm," she said. The corners of her lips turned up into an almost-smile.

"Look, what I'm saying is, we weren't ready...we weren't *nearly* ready, and we're still way not ready. I know you have super powers or whatever, and actually, I have a lot of questions about that, because the wizard got a little weird when he talked about your mutant power thi—sorry! Sorry. Not your mutant power thing, you know, but..." Virgil took a deep breath and started over. "What I am saying is that we're going to come back, and we're going to rock that demon's world, and we're going to banish him so hard, he'll blast straight down into the eighty-eighth circle of hell. But it's not happening tonight." He frowned down at his hand and flexed his fingers. "I can't even make magic happen without a bracelet."

Abby rubbed her forehead. She glanced helplessly back at the house. There was a quick flutter of motion from one of the windows, and a curtain fell into place, as if someone had been watching them from inside. "Okay," she finally said, turning back and glancing at Simon across the street. "You're right. We'll come back when we have a plan."

"Good. Thank you," Virgil said, sounding relieved. "Simon had that serious 'I'll leave you behind and you can Uber home' look in his eyes."

"Does he leave you behind a lot?" Abby asked, raising an eyebrow.

"Well, sometimes," Virgil shrugged. Then he grinned. "But only when I deserve it."

He turned and walked back across the lawn, heading toward Simon and the Pontiac. Abby took a couple of steps, then she paused. She glanced back at the house, with its blood-red windows and dripping black flowers. Then she made a quick decision: she grabbed the locket around her neck and pulled down sharply, snapping the thin silver chain that held it around her neck. She made sure neither Simon nor Virgil was looking in her direction, and she dropped the necklace into the grass.

Then she hurried across the lawn, catching up with Virgil and walking back with him toward Simon's car.

CHAPTER 17

"Everything okay?" Simon asked as they approached the Pontiac.

"I was about to ask you the same question," Virgil replied. "You good?"

Simon nodded. "Yeah. I'm good."

Abby sidled up next to Simon, her hands planted in her back pockets. She leaned up against the Pontiac, her hip pressing against the fender. "Guess we should call it a night?" she said.

Simon nodded slowly. "Guess so," he said, sounding a little reluctant. Abby had a feeling it had more to do with saying goodbye to her for the evening than it did with saying goodbye to Asag.

"I work a double shift tomorrow," she told them. "You guys coming in?"

"Let me ask you a question...you know any secret cheat codes for any of the games that make them spit out extra tickets?" Virgil asked hopefully. "I have been playing for that stupid Nerf gun for so, so long..."

Abby snickered. "Sorry, champ," she said, pushing herself off the car. "You'll have to earn it like all the other suckers."

"We have to be at Llewyn's early tomorrow," Simon said. Then he added, "But...maybe we can come by after." He gave Virgil a questioning look.

Virgil nodded. "Definitely."

Abby smiled. "Good," she decided. She touched Simon's arm as she scooted between them, taking a few steps toward her truck. "See you tomorrow, then."

Simon was grateful for the darkness; it meant Abby wouldn't be able to tell how hard he was blushing. "Tomorrow," he confirmed.

"I'll be there too, but, you know, whatever," Virgil said, rolling his eyes at the other two.

"Get home safely," Simon said.

"No promises," Abby teased. She scratched her neck, and then her fingers began to move around her throat, patting her skin, as if searching for something that wasn't there.

"Everything okay?" Simon asked.

"Skin mites?" Virgil suggested.

"My necklace. I must have dropped it by the tree," Abby said, pursing her lips into a pout.

"We can go look," Simon said, taking a step back into the road.

"No. Thank you. But no. Go home." Abby smiled again, and it lit up her entire face. It seemed to light up Simon's face, too. "I'll find it. Go on back, I'll see you guys tomorrow."

"Okay," Simon said, returning her smile. "Sounds good." He pulled open the driver's side door and almost caught himself in the shoulder with the corner of it. He jerked to the side, narrowly missing the edge, and then he blushed again. "See you tomorrow."

"Right, we got it, everyone will see everyone tomorrow," Virgil said, shaking his head. He jumped into the passenger seat and twirled his finger. "Let's do this. I've got a frozen burrito with my name on it at home."

Simon gave Abby a nod, then he got into the car, too, and with one last wave, they pulled away from the curb, drifted down the street, and disappeared around the corner.

Abby watched them go. She smiled to herself as she shook her head and crossed back toward Mrs. Grunberg's house. Simon really was very sweet, she decided. She tried not to make too many personal connections, as a general rule, but there was something about him she liked.

Something she really, really liked.

She hopped back up onto the sidewalk, stepped back into the lawn, picked up her necklace, and stuffed it into her pocket. She looked up and down the block, but didn't see anyone looking her way. Satisfied that she was alone, she zipped up her jacket, pulled up her hood, and slunk into the shadows that stretched and dripped from the side of Mrs. Grunberg's house.

CHAPTER 18

Virgil yawned and stretched and glared sourly toward the sun. "It's so early," he whined.

"You know most people are, like, showered and dressed and already at work by now," Simon pointed out.

"Yeah. Well." Virgil spat into the drainage ditch. "Those people aren't me."

Simon offered Virgil a coffee, and Virgil eyed it suspiciously. "It's coffee," Simon said. "It'll help."

"It's bitter, and it's terrible, and I don't drink coffee, because I'm not a 50-year-old chain-smoking journalist," Virgil shot back. But he reached out and took the cup anyway, and he took a sip. "Ugh," he said, his face going sour. "Terrible." He took another sip anyway.

"It'll grow on you," Simon promised.

They shuffled toward the tent beneath the bridge. Everything was as they had left it the night before. The tin can was still perched atop the old, partially-melted shopping cart.

"So do we, like, *knock?*" Virgil asked.

"How do you know on a tent?"

Virgil shrugged. "I don't know...you're the smart one. I'm just here for the color commentary."

They crept up to the flap of the tent. Simon reached out, took the edge of the flap gingerly, and peeled it back. Inside, the tent was dark. "Hello?" he called into the space.

There was no reply.

"Maybe he's dead," Virgil suggested.

"Why would you say that?" Simon asked, dropping the tent flap and straightening up. "What's the matter with you?"

"People die, dude," Virgil said, giving Simon a shrug. "Circle of life."

"I know," Simon glowered.

Virgil shrank back, suddenly guilty. "Sorry," he said quietly. "I'm not feeling so sharp today. I'll drink more coffee."

"You do that."

Simon crouched down and pulled back the tent flap again. "Hello?" he called a second time, but there was still no response. He looked up at Virgil. "I guess we just...go in?"

"We *were* invited," Virgil pointed out. "Even under vampire rules, we would have a right to go inside."

"Good point." Simon crawled forward, squinting into the tent. It was just so completely, utterly dark inside. "All right. Let's go."

He took a step forward. His face slammed into a solid wall.

"Ow!" he cried, falling back. He rubbed his nose, then stared incredulously at the tent. "What the...?"

"Boy, you are *really* bad at going inside tents," Virgil observed. He approached the flap and pulled back the canvas. He reached forward, and his hand made it about three inches past the flaps before it pushed up against a solid surface. "Or maybe the tent's really bad at letting people in..."

He moved his hand along the surface of the wall, and he couldn't tell if it was invisible, or if it was solid black. Either way, though, it covered the entire opening to the tent, stretching from one end to the other, and from the ground all the way to the pitched ceiling. He pressed both hands against the wall and pushed. It didn't give a centimeter. "Well, that's weird," Virgil decided.

"I guess that's how you knock on a tent," Simon said. He hopped back up to his feet and closed his hand into a fist. He knocked gently on the wall. Even though he touched it only lightly, the sound of his knock reverberated loudly behind the wall, through the tent. It sounded as if someone inside was slamming a sledgehammer against stone walls. It was such a startling sound that Simon and Virgil both jumped back. They watched as a thin line of blue light appeared along the wall, splitting it horizontally in half. The light widened, reaching both upward and downward, becoming a wide bar of light. As it continued its outward growth, the center began to dissolve away, so that as they watched, the light seemed to wipe away the wall, from the center, and soon it disappeared completely, revealing the inside of the tent as they remembered it; the grand entryway with its stone floor and wood-beam walls, opening up into the expansive sitting room beyond.

Llewyn the wizard stood in the center of the foyer, his arms resting on the handle of a massive axe. It was the size of a fully-grown man, with a double-sided blade that was about the size of two large hams tied together. The handle was as thick as a small tree trunk. The metal head was on the floor, with the handle sticking straight up, reaching up to Llewyn's chest. His arms were crossed atop the end of the wood. "Welcome back," he said.

His blue eye was covered by a leather patch, which Simon and Virgil both found somehow comforting. The blue light that emanated from his empty socket wasn't exactly the most pleasant sight.

"Um...thanks," Simon said lamely. He nudged Virgil.

"Yeah, thanks," Virgil added.

The sorcerer grinned. He was fully aware of his effect on the young men, and he seemed to relish it. He lifted up the axe with a grunt, turning it over in his hands and giving it a practice swing. "Shall we begin?"

Simon swallowed hard. "Are we...going to use that?" he asked, nodding at the axe.

"*I'm* going to use it," Llewyn corrected him, hefting the weapon. "You're going to try not to be killed by it."

"Sounds like a blast," Virgil muttered. He took another sip of coffee. "Pretty glad we came."

Llewyn beckoned them to follow him, then turned and headed deeper into the tent. The two young men stepped inside, closing the flaps behind them. The wall reformed, this time from the top and bottom of the opening, re-sealing itself until its two blue light lines met in the middle. The bars of light left behind a solid wall that looked like acrylic, or Saran wrap. They could see through it clearly, they could see the tent flaps on the other side, and the sliver of concrete drainage ditch that was visible between them. Simon shook his head in wonder. He supposed nothing should really surprise him, given the fact that they were in the home of a powerful wizard.

Even so, a certain amount of un-reality, he decided, was always going to be a bit surprising.

They followed Llewyn across the sitting room and back down the hallway at the other end. But this time, the sorcerer stopped halfway down the hall and went through one of the doors on his right. They followed him in, expecting to see another room, or chamber...but instead, they saw another long hallway, this one also lined with doors on both sides. The hall looked exactly like the one they had just come down.

"Should we be leaving bread crumbs behind?" Virgil murmured under his breath.

"I've seen horror movies that start like this," Simon replied.

"I've seen horror movies that *end* like this," Virgil countered.

They gave each other a look. Then they continued on after the sorcerer.

After three more doors, and three more hallways, they finally passed through into a room...although calling it a "room" wasn't exactly right. It had a stone floor, and stone walls that reached up and curved overhead, meeting high above them in a cupola, like the ceiling of a cathedral. But the room was *humongous* and styled to look like the outdoors, with wide patches of mossy grass growing over the stones on the floor, and with great, old oak trees thrusting up from the ground and stretching toward the ceiling with their wide, leafy branches. Smaller bushes and shrubs dotted the landscape, too, and the stone walls took on a blueish color as they reached up toward the curved ceiling, giving the visual impression that they were outside, in an open field of trees on a pleasant, blue-sky day.

"Do you think they sell this tent on Amazon? I am totally getting one," Virgil decided.

Llewyn strode out into a wide clearing, situated amidst a circle of trees. He gave the giant axe a few windmill swings, then he slung it into the trunk of one of the trees. The blade sank in halfway, and the trunk held the axe in place. Then he returned to the center of the clearing. He moved his hands over the spongy grass, and three tendrils sprang up from the moss, growing like flowers in time-lapse films. They curled and uncurled, growing taller and taller, and thicker, too, until they came up to Llewyn's waist. Each one swelled with a blossom colored in a different shade of blue, each of the blossoms as large as a fist and closed up as tightly as one, too. They formed a sort of a living fence between the two young men and the wizard, waving lazily back and forth as if swaying in a breeze.

Or as if they were being charmed like snakes.

"Come," the sorcerer beckoned, throwing off his coat and tossing it aside. A pair of scraggly branches dropped down from the canopy overhead and caught the coat in midair, then hauled it up so it disappeared in the greenery near the ceiling. Llewyn pushed up the sleeves of his white shirt and motioned them closer. "We've got a lot to do."

CHAPTER 19

"Are we practicing to become gardeners?" Virgil asked, looking doubtfully down at the closed-up flowers.

Llewyn grunted. "More than you know," he said with a grin. "Yesterday, I showed you that you have magic. Today, you start learning how to *use* that magic. Eventually, you'll build up enough strength and control to confront Asag." When he said this, Simon detected a note of regret in his voice, and it occurred to him that in addition to being frustrated with the fact that he had to focus so much of his power on the sharp black thing in his chest to keep it from splitting open his heart, Llewyn might actually be disappointed that he didn't have enough reserve power to face Asag himself.

As if it were some kind of sport.

If you're strong enough, I guess it does become some kind of sport, Simon realized.

He had an idea what Asag was capable of. It gave him chills to think about how strong Llewyn's unbridled power must be, if he could think of a cage match with that immortal hell-spawn as a game.

"Until you learn how to augment and manage your powers," Llewyn continued, "you will practice different ways to contain them, and to put them to use." He swept a hand over the blossoms. "We start that part of your training today."

"We're going to power-blast the flowers?" Virgil asked.

"No," Llewyn said, shaking his head. "You're done power-blasting for a while."

"But—"

"No," the wizard said again, this time with a heavy note of finality. "Not until you control it." He set his mouth into a hard line and crossed his arm. "Your misfire *was* on the news last night. Channel 5."

Virgil gulped. He laughed nervously. "Well, at least it wasn't CNN," he said.

"It might have been, for all I know," Llewyn grunted. He shook his head ruefully. "I don't have cable."

"We could check the intern—" Virgil started, but Simon silenced him with a look. Virgil nodded. "Right. Sorry. No power blasts."

Llewyn gestured down at the three writhing flowers. "These are curiocus plants. Every novitiate of the Seventh Order starts their journey with the curiocus. The selection is a ritual that began thousands of years ago, with the first mages of the Forgotten Lands. With the cultivation of your curioci, you take a step that leaves a footprint you cannot clear. Whether you see this through to mage level, or abandon your pursuit tomorrow, you will have unlocked something that will be both a strength and a curse to you. Knowledge is power, and knowledge of your own power is a heavy weight to bear. From this point, there is no turning back. This is your final opportunity to withdraw with your innocence intact. If you approach the curioci, your path is set. Do you have any questions?"

Virgil raised his hand awkwardly. "What's a 'novitiate'?"

The wizard sighed. "Any *other* questions?"

Simon couldn't deny a certain feeling of fear that was growing in the pit of his stomach. Just a few days ago, he had been a regular guy, living a regular life in a mostly-regular city, give or take all the supernatural happenings. But now the veil had been pulled back; he had met a wizard and an empath, he had discovered the powers of magic within himself, he had felt the darkness, and he had seen the literal face of evil.

His view of Templar was beginning to widen; now it wasn't just a city nestled against the Appalachians. Llewyn had enlightened him, and Asag had, too...and Abby: the town was also a battlefield of the supernatural war between the forces of Good and Evil. He and Virgil had stumbled willingly, if ignorantly, into that war, and they had chosen a side. It was the right side to be on, but that didn't make the war any less frightening.

But it was a war worth fighting.

And he had already lost his sister in a secret battle in that war. He hadn't known it then, but he was sure of it now. Laura was an innocent victim of the psychic struggle for Templar.

He couldn't do anything to save her then. But he could do something to avenge her now.

And he couldn't save his own sister, but maybe he could save someone else's. He could help stem the flow of losses in this ongoing struggle.

"We're in," he said.

Llewyn looked at him, considering him carefully. Then he gave Simon a solemn nod. "Good," he said. "Then let's begin."

The two young men cautiously approached the flowers. When they were just a few feet away, the wizard held up his hands for them to stop. They did.

"The fruit of the curiocus hasn't yet formed," he said, holding his hand over the flower in the middle. It snaked up closer toward his palm, almost as if it were sniffing his skin, like a dog would. "The fruit that is born from your curiocus will be your own curio, an artifact that is powerful and bound to you, that is useful to only you, and to no one else. It will be made expressly for you; the curiocus will bond with your past, and with your spirit."

"So it's like choosing a wand in *Harry Potter*," Virgil said.

Llewyn shot him a look. His glowing eye burned so brightly that they could see the light through the thick leather of the eyepatch. "It is not like choosing a wand in *Harry Potter*," he gruffed. "It is very, very different."

"It doesn't sound very different."

Llewyn frowned and turned to Simon. "Is he always like this?" he asked.

Simon nodded. "Pretty much always, yeah."

The wizard re-centered himself over the middle curiocus. "Watch," he instructed. He closed his eye and placed both hands around the navy blue petals of the closed flower. The flower immediately expanded to fill the space between his palms. It swelled, filling from the inside like a balloon, pushing against his hands and expanding in all directions until the blossom was the size of a bocce ball. It broke free of its stem. Then the wizard was holding the bulbous blossom in his cupped hands. The petals fell away, one by one, until the entire flower had broken apart, revealing the thing it had grown inside: a flask, about the size of the wizard's great fist, made from leather of some sort, or perhaps from some animal's bladder. It looked ancient, well-worn, scraped and stained with age.

"Your patronus is a flask?" Virgil asked, surprised.

"You're confusing your Harry Potter," Simon said, rolling his eyes.

"I haven't seen those movies in a long time," Virgil admitted.

Llewyn ran his fingers over the old flask, touching it gently and with care. His eye softened with memory. "My great-grandfather had a flask like this," he said, lost in some secret remembrance. "He was a mage from the Scottish Highlands. Always had it full of his homemade atholl brose. Do you know the atholl brose drink?"

The two young men shook their heads.

"No. Not many do these days." The wizard smiled at the flask. "This is a powerful curio indeed." He closed his other hand over it, mostly concealing it from sight. The flask shone with a bright white light, and then it was gone, disappearing into the ether.

"Where did it go?" Simon asked. He reminded himself again that nothing the wizard did should surprise him.

He hoped magic would always be amazing to him. He wondered if he would ever take it for granted.

"I've placed it in my psychic castle," Llewyn replied, grinning broadly, fully aware of the long series of questions this was sure to set off in his apprentices' minds. "All in due time," he said, preempting those questions. "First...let's discover your curios."

"What if we choose the wrong one?" Simon asked doubtfully.

But the wizard shook his head. "That's not how it works. As I said, you don't choose them; they choose you."

"Like Hogwarts wands," Virgil whispered to Simon again.

Llewyn closed his eyes and took a breath. He decided to let it go. "All you need to do is choose a blossom. Pick a shade of blue that's particularly attractive to you, if it helps. Place your hands over it, and be still. The curiocus will do the rest."

Simon bobbed his head thoughtfully. "Makes sense, I guess. Or as much sense as any of this makes."

"Question," Virgil said, raising a hand in the air. "What do we do with the curios once we have them?"

The wizard grunted. "You'll see."

Virgil raised his eyebrow at Simon. "You want to go first?" he asked.

Simon gestured forward with one hand. "Be my guest," he replied.

Virgil took a deep breath. Then he stepped forward, up to the line of flowers. He chose the one on the right, a midnight blue blossom. He lowered his hands over the flower, then looked at Llewyn for confirmation that he was doing it correctly. The wizard nodded, so Virgil closed his eyes and tried to quiet his mind.

For a few seconds, nothing happened. But then he felt a strange coolness against his palms, as if they were being caressed with a cold breeze. Then he felt the brush of flower petals, a gentle nudge that turned into a strong push as the flower grew bigger and bigger. His hands moved out as the blossom expanded, and soon it was growing through and above his palms. He peeked down and watched it balloon outward. It grew larger than Llewyn's had, and this gave him a small, if petty, feeling of pride. Then the flower broke off of its stem, and Virgil was cradling the curiocus in his hands.

It was heavy, heavier than he thought any flower could be. He hefted it a few times, and the weight felt somehow familiar...

The petals began to fall away, drifting down to the mossy green floor of the forest room. It only took a few seconds for all of the petals to fall, leaving Virgil holding his curio.

It was a vintage wooden Skee-Ball ball, nicked and worn with use and time.

Virgil gaped at the ball. He twisted his palms over it, feeling the texture under his skin, letting the oils from his hands soak into the surface of the wood. He lifted his eyes and looked quizzically at Llewyn. "How did you know?" he asked.

"I didn't. The curiocus did." The wizard stepped closer and inspected the wooden ball. "It's a fine specimen," he admitted, "though I haven't the slightest idea what it's for."

"Skee-Ball," Virgil said absently, inspecting the ball. He had never seen one so old, or so well-formed. "We'll show you how to play sometime."

"I trust it holds a significance for you?" Llewyn asked.

"You literally couldn't find anything on Earth that holds *more* significance for him," Simon laughed.

Virgil shrugged. When Simon was right, he was right.

"What do I do with it?" he asked.

"In a moment," Llewyn replied. He crooked one finger and beckoned Simon forward. "Your turn."

Simon nodded. "Okay." He stepped up to the last remaining flower. It had a striking cornflower blue blossom. The color of it seemed both cheerful and powerful at the same time. He liked that.

He placed his hands over the flower, and he closed his eyes. He tried to clear his mind. It was harder than he thought it would be; images kept shouldering their way into his vision of their own accord, without his conjuring them up. But he decided that was okay; if the curiocus was supposed to tap into the very essence of you, then maybe it was okay to show the flower what it was that kept you going.

The usual images cropped up: flashes of his parents, of his childhood, of him and Virgil playing in the woods and running through the Templar alleys; pictures of his dad, pictures of Laura, pictures of Abby...and something deeper, something darker, a picture that was mostly reds and blacks, a heavy and despairing thing that he actively worked to push down, because he knew if he let it bob to the surface, it would show him a porcelain baby mask, or maybe the nightmare face beneath it.

He jumped with surprise when he felt the flower's petals pushing against his palms. Then he relaxed, focused in on a mental image of Laura's gravestone, white, shining granite against an emerald green field, and the flower grew and grew and grew, until he was holding the blossom in his hands, free of its stem, full of the fruit that would be his own personal curio.

The cornflower petals began to fall away. Simon looked down into his hands.

He was holding a key. It was antique, with an ornate metal scrollwork bow, a channeled throat, and a jagged bit with five mismatched teeth.

"A fine key," Llewyn said approvingly. "What does it open?"

Simon gazed down at the thing in his hand. "I have no idea," he whispered, turning the key over between his fingers. "I have absolutely no idea."

The wizard furrowed his brow. "It has no significance for you?" he asked, sounding concerned.

"Not that I can think of," Simon said, confused. He squinted down at the key, even held it up to the light, trying to get a better look. Its shape was entirely unfamiliar. As far as he could recall, he had never even *held* a key that wasn't a standard Schlage-style key, modern, simple, and unremarkable.

But *this* key...this key was extraordinary.

"I should recognize it, right?" Simon asked, a feeling of panic starting to rise in his throat. "If it's my curio, it's something that should be important to me, I should know what it *is*, shouldn't I?"

Llewyn rubbed his chin. "The curiocus knows. This key is significant to you. It is surprising that you don't know why, or don't remember. But it is yours; that much is very clear. The curiocus is never wrong." He placed his great hand over Simon's so that the key was pinned between their two palms. He looked at Simon with a heavy gravity. "If it doesn't open a door to your past, it'll open a door to your future. Keep it sacred. Keep it safe."

Simon nodded. He would keep it sacred. He would keep it safe.

He just wished he knew why.

"I have a hunch about what it might be," Llewyn said, using his own hand to close Simon's fingers over the key. "Give it time. If it doesn't reveal its secrets, then you and I will force its hand. Together."

Simon exhaled. Having the wizard on his side lifted a weight from his chest. "Thank you," he said.

The wizard winked his one good eye.

"Okay, so what do we do now?" Virgil asked, inspecting his Skee-Ball artifact.

"The curio chose you; now you must reciprocate the choice by imbuing it with your energy," the wizard said. "This will be your first and most potent article of power."

"I've got to be honest, I have no idea what that means," Virgil pointed out.

"We're...new at this," Simon reminded the wizard.

Llewyn took a deep breath. It had been over a century since he'd trained apprentices. He took a deep breath. "When you have a curio, you can take some of your magic and transfer it to the object. Then, that magic lives in there. And when you need it, you can call it forth, and the object will expend its power according to your designs."

Virgil cleared his throat. "Am I crazy, or did that not clear it up very much?" he asked sincerely.

Llewyn's cheeks grew dark. "Follow my instructions, and you'll see," he said between clenched teeth. "Remember how you focused your energy in your manacles?" They both nodded. "The same process is in effect here. Gather your strength...focus your memories...feel your energy...push it into the curio."

Simon stepped forward, holding his key before him. He closed his eyes and formed the now-familiar burning down deep in his stomach. He forced it up into his chest, pushed it out through his arm, and gathered it into his palm. The key began to hum with its own power, and it vibrated in Simon's hand. Then suddenly, the warmth and strength evaporated from his skin, his magic completely subsided, and Simon was left with nothing but an old skeleton key sitting in his upturned hand.

But the key had changed. It had felt the magic.

And more than having felt it, it had actually soaked it in; Simon could see that clearly. Even though the key didn't exactly glow, it did seem to have a heightened sense of self-importance. It was a little bit shinier, and a little bit brighter, and a little bit prouder, and a little bit heavier. Simon pinched it between two fingers and held it up in the false light of the forest chamber, inspecting it carefully. "It's different," he said aloud.

"It's pretty shiny," Virgil observed, stepping up and inspecting the key from up close. "Not bad."

"It will be a token of incredible importance," Llewyn said. "Mark my words. Keep it safe. It will one day do the same for you."

Simon frowned down at his key. He hoped that the wizard's words were true.

"Now you," Llewyn said, nodding toward Virgil. "Ready to transfer your magic?"

"I'm a magic-transferring expert," Virgil replied. He held the wooden ball up high in the air, closed his eyes, and thought about how much he wanted to win enough Skee-Ball tickets to get that coveted Nerf gun. He didn't know how long he'd have to work, but he did know that this was exactly this sort of ball that could carry him across the finish line. He had worked at mastering Skee-Ball for almost a whole decade. He and the wooden ball understood each other. They were practically one. And while he felt bad that Simon had wasted his mental energy on conjuring up a key to nowhere, Virgil felt confident that he and the Skee-Ball ball were always meant to be together. He held the ball tightly in his hands, and he closed his eyes. He, too, brought forward the same memories he'd conjured when he had charged his manacle, all the easy spots of brightness he could recall. He pushed the ball of heat up into his chest, out beyond his shoulders and into his arms, and he could actually feel the magic seeping into the wooden ball. He could feel it become saturated with an otherworldly strength. And when he opened his eyes, he saw the distinct difference in his artifact: it had become golden, and full of a strange, internal light.

It was its own being now, its own creature. Bonded to Virgil, but wholly separate.

Virgil held the glowing wooden ball out toward Llewyn. "Magic-transferring expert," he said again.

The wizard smirked. "A fine job," he admitted. "These curios are the things that will serve you for as long as you live. In your darkest hours, they will rise to your aid."

"That's pretty cool," Virgil admitted, admiring his wooden ball. "But how do they work?"

"Each curio is different. My great-grandfather's flask will work differently than your ball, and they'll both work differently than the key. The flask may always be filled with water, no matter how much you drink...or perhaps any liquid it holds gives the drinker some extra burst of strength or stamina. It will be impossible to say, until I've had the time to work with it, to learn its magic. You'll need to learn how your own curios work."

"Pretty sure mine works like a Skee-Ball," Virgil said. He took a few steps and pitched the wooden ball underhand across the clearing. It rocketed along the mossy grass, actually *gaining* speed the further it got from Virgil, and glowing its golden light. It zoomed toward one of the trees and struck it head-on, exploding through the thick trunk and ricocheting off the stone wall on the far side. It shot back across the room, knocked against the opposite wall, then screamed back toward Virgil. He shrieked in fear and threw up his hands to block his face, and the wooden ball came to a sudden stop, right against his palm. Virgil peeked through his fingers. The ball hovered in the air, waiting patiently for him to grab it. He did, and the golden light dimmed.

Virgil cleared his throat. "Well. Guess that's what *that* does."

"Indeed," the wizard said. He turned to Simon and considered the key. "Yours...may work differently."

"Yeah, I figured that," Simon frowned.

"As I said," the wizard continued, crossing his arms, "you can call upon your curio when you need it. When you *don't* need it, it should be kept safe. A lost or stolen curio is a dangerous thing. In the wrong hands..." His words drifted off as he considered some hidden horror. "You don't want them in the wrong hands," he finished.

"Should we get, like, a safe for the apartment?" Virgil asked.

"You'll store it in your psychic vault," Llewyn replied.

Simon and Virgil both raised their eyebrows at that one. "Our psychic vault?" they asked in unison.

"It's a place that exists on the astral plane. A six-dimensional space that you create, and that only you can access."

Simon scratched the side of his neck. "I know we've seen a *lot* of insane things of the last few days, and between demons and wizards and shadow flowers and possessed Skee-Balls, I shouldn't really get stuck on 'astral plane,' but...seriously? The astral plane?"

"It's not theoretical, if that's what you're suggesting," the wizard said, sounding a little irritated. "And it's far from the only other plane that exists beyond our own reality." Then he grinned, a sharp, dangerous smile that sent a shiver down Simon's spine. "Perhaps you'll even visit it yourself one day."

"Okay, okay, so how do we create these psychic vaults?" Virgil asked, desperate to break the tension.

"You've already created them," Llewyn replied.

"What? We did?" Simon asked. "When?"

"In the future."

Simon wrinkled up his face in confusion. "We already created them in the future?"

"Yes," the wizard said, as if this should be obvious.

"That doesn't make any sense."

"Not in this level of reality. But on the astral plane, time works differently. Or, to be more exact, time does not exist, at least not as we understand it. On the astral plane, time isn't a line, or a circle, or a ribbon. It's a hailstorm."

"*That* doesn't make any sense, either," Virgil pointed out.

The wizard smirked. "There are plenty who would say the concept of time in a line is absurd."

"Those people should probably get a watch."

"Wait, I'm sorry, can we go back a second?" Simon interrupted. "So our psychic vaults already exist, because at some point in the future, we will create them. But if they're already created now, why would we need to create them in the future? They already exist. It's like if you already have a cake, you wouldn't bake a cake so you could then have a cake. You already have the cake."

"Man, I could go for cake right now," Virgil said wistfully.

Simon ignored him. He was getting a little worked up about the hailstorm of time. "Having a psychic vault means that in the future we'll have to make one, but we won't ever need to make one because we already have one. So when will we make one?"

"You won't," Llewyn shrugged. "You already have one."

"But if I never make one, how will I have one now?!"

"Because you've already made it."

"But I haven't!"

"But you will."

"But I won't!"

"You won't need to."

Simon screamed. He pulled at the roots of his hair and turned away. He walked over to the trees, to put some distance between himself and the argument that was warping his brain.

"Makes sense to me," Virgil said. "But I'm a lot smarter than Simon."

"No you're not," Simon said from across the room.

"Don't think about it too much," the wizard suggested. "We've got a lot more to worry about. And trust me, there's plenty about the kinesthetic arts that makes less sense than this."

"Great," Simon muttered into the trees.

Virgil gave his wooden ball a few light tosses into the air. "So how do we store these bad boys?" he asked. "If I hold onto this for much longer, I'm going to want to break more stuff."

The wizard nodded. "Finding your vault is easy. All you have to do is picture it in your mind."

"But we don't know what they look like!" Simon cried, exasperated. He was circling the room from beyond the trees.

"Yes, you do," Llewyn replied. "You know because you built it." The wizard turned his attention to Virgil. "Trust me on this."

"Oh, I do," Virgil assured him. "You taught me how to shoot lasers from my wrist and grow a magic Skee-Ball from a flower. Whatever you're selling, I'm buying."

Llewyn smirked. "Good." He raised his voice so Simon could hear him clearly, too. "Picture a vault in your mind. Whatever the vault looks like is the right way for it to look."

Simon sighed. He sulked back over toward them, his mind racing with the strangeness of life. "Okay," he said, defeated. "Okay." He closed his eyes. "I'm picturing a vault. Now what?"

"Now open it."

"In my mind?" he asked without opening his eyes.

"Yes."

"I can't, it's locked," Virgil said, his eyes also squeezed tightly shut.

"What sort of lock is it?" Llewyn asked, and somewhere in the furthest reaches of Simon's mind, he had a spark of understanding about just how absurd this conversation would sound to someone who was eavesdropping.

"It's a combination lock."

"Mine has a keypad," Simon sighed, giving into the ridiculousness of the exercise. He let himself imagine a vault, huge and round, like an old bank vault, but shiny and new. A small keypad was set into the door above the handle—black buttons with white numbers spaced out in two rows, zero through four on top and five through nine on the bottom. In Simon's imagination, the vault was set into a white background. It wasn't a wall. It was more like a void. Like a brilliant, white nothingness.

"Numbers," the sorcerer nodded. "Good. You already know the combinations for your vaults. Enter the combination, and open the door."

"This is so stupid," Simon muttered. Then, louder, he asked, "How do I know the combination?"

"It's the combination you gave it in the future."

Simon thought his head might explode.

"Oh, super easy!" Virgil chirped happily. "One left, one right, one left. Bam!"

The wizard frowned. "You made your combination one-one-one?"

"Pretty easy to remember, huh?" The vault in Virgil's mind was a tall, slender safe, about the size and shape of a grandfather clock. He spun the dial on the combination lock, and the bolt fell back. He imagined pulling open the door. Even though the outside of the vault was only about a foot deep, on the inside, the vault looked infinite. "Cool," he breathed.

Simon sighed. *This is so stupid,* he thought. He could see the keypad clearly enough, and that actually surprised him. He wasn't known for being the most imaginative guy on the block, but he saw his psychic vault with an impressive clarity. It really looked like he could reach out and touch the numbers on the keypad.

Of course, that didn't help him to know what numbers he was *supposed* to touch on the keypad.

"So I already know the combination, and I should just punch in the numbers I already know that I'll give myself some day in the future, even though I won't actually give them to myself in the future because I'll already have had them in mind in the past."

Llewyn nodded. "Yes."

Simon sighed again. *So, so stupid.* Keeping his eyes closed, he shook out his hands, as if he was going to actually use them to touch the imaginary keypad, and as if the stakes were somehow very high. He assumed they probably were not. If you type in the wrong imaginary numbers on an imaginary keypad, what was the worst that could happen? You reset and start over again, right?

"By the way, if you get them wrong, your psychic vault might lock forever," Llewyn said, as if reading his mind. "That could have some serious mental repercussions for you. Given the complexities of the astral plane and all."

Simon frowned. "Thanks a lot."

Llewyn touched a finger to his forehead and tipped it toward his apprentice. "I'm here to educate," he said.

Screw it, Simon thought. *If I don't know them now, it's not like I'll know them in the future. And if I really did set them in the future, then future me better have remembered what present me does and doesn't know.* He imagined himself reaching out and pressing the numbers on the imaginary buttons that were set into the imaginary vault. He just let his hand guide itself, let it press the numbers that it seemed to want to press.

6-0-6-2-1.

The keypad beeped. A green light came on. The vault unlocked. The door swung open.

"Whoa. I did it," Simon said, watching the psychic vault fall open. His, too, was infinite inside, with endless shelves lining the walls, which curved into a circle, the same shape as the big vault door.

"Nice! What was your code?" Virgil asked, slapping his friend on the back.

Simon shrugged. "Just some random numbers. 6-0-6-2-1."

Virgil snorted. "Those aren't random, dummy."

"They're not?"

"No! They're your birthday, and Laura's birthday; yours is June sixth, and Laura's is June twenty-first."

"Numbers have meaning," Llewyn said sagely, his one eye gleaming.

"Huh," Simon said, opening his eyes and blinking. "Well, what do you know about that?"

"The next step is to place your curios inside your vault," the sorcerer said, getting them back on track.

"Yeah, I was wondering about that," Virgil said, scratching his chin. "If the vaults are in our heads, and the curios are in our hands, how do we…?" A terrible thought crossed his mind then, and he gulped. "We don't *actually* put the curios *into* our heads…?"

Llewyn sighed. "No. You don't put the curios into your heads. You hold them in your hands, and you focus your energies on them, just like you did with the flowers. Just like you did with the manacles. *Focus*. Once you feel the magic flowing between you and the artifact, call up the psychic image of your vault, and imagine yourself placing it inside."

Virgil laughed. "Sesame Street always told me that my imagination was magical, but I didn't think they meant it *literally*," he said. He closed his eyes and concentrated on his wooden ball. He pushed the magic up from his gut once again, sending it through his arms, so that it pooled inside the ball. He pictured his tall, opened vault, and he imagined himself placing the ball inside the cabinet. Then he closed the imaginary door and locked it.

He opened his eyes. The wooden ball had disappeared.

"Whoa," he breathed, his eyes glowing with excitement. "That is *wild*." He nudged Simon, flashing him a grin. "You gotta try it."

Simon frowned, but he set to work. He readjusted his feet so that he felt more firm, standing on the spongy grass, and then he closed his eyes. He pushed his magic up and into his hands, holding the key tightly and feeling the energy flow into its small, metal form. Then he pictured his own vault, and imagined himself placing the key inside, on the top shelf on the left side. Then he closed the vault, and the lock clunked as it slid into place.

When he opened his eyes, they key was gone.

"Very good," Llewyn said, his voice actually filling with something that sounded like pride. "You have a true aptitude for magic. Both of you."

"Aw, shucks," Virgil said, giving Simon a wink. "We're good at stuff!"

"You'll both make fine mages someday," Llewyn admitted with a grin. Then he quickly added, "Someday far, far down the road."

"So the curio just...*sits* there?" Simon asked.

The wizard nodded. "Until you retrieve it. Until you return to your psychic vault, open it, and take the artifact out. When you do, it will appear in your hands again." He gave them a grin. "Like magic."

"Man," Virgil said, shaking his head. "Life is just so, so cool now."

Simon nodded over toward the axe that was wedged deeply into the trunk of the tree not far away. "When do we start working with that?" he asked nervously. The handle of the axe alone was as tall as he was, and the double-edged blade was about as wide as his shoulders.

It was an incredibly imposing weapon.

Llewyn smirked. "We've come to the axe now, as a matter of fact," he said, striding across the clearing and wrenching it from the tree. He reached down and touched the deep channel he had cut into the trunk, and his lips moved. The tree began to heal itself from the inside out, filling back in and covering with bark until there was no wound to speak of at all. When he did this, the hole that Virgil's Skee-Ball curio had blown through the other tree across the way also healed itself from the inside, and within seconds, both trees were fully restored and healthy. Then the wizard marched back over to where the two young men stood, and he held the axe up high, so they could get a good look.

"Yes, we start with the axe now," he repeated, glancing down at them with mischief in his eye.

Then he gripped the axe with both hands and swung it down at Virgil's neck as hard as he could.

CHAPTER 20

"Oh, nice," Simon said grumpily, crossing his arms in annoyance. "You killed Virgil."

Virgil's body lay on the spongy ground in a heap. Simon nudged it with his toe.

"I didn't even touch him," the wizard protested, still holding the axe mid-air, at the spot he had stopped his downward swing, right before Virgil had shrieked with fear and fainted. "I was making a demonstration."

"You demonstrated too well," Simon pointed out. He gave Virgil a gentle kick. "Hey. Wake up."

Virgil's eyes fluttered open. His head lolled from side to side on the ground. "What happened?" he asked. Then his eyes opened wide with memory, and his hands flew to his neck, feeling for the axe wound he was sure he would find there. "Am I dead? Am I a ghost? Oh man, I'm a ghost, you made me a ghost so I can fight the demon without dying, didn't you? *Didn't you?!*"

"Virgil, calm down," Simon said, reaching down and grabbing his friend under the elbow. He hauled Virgil to his feet and brushed off his back. "You're not dead. You just fainted."

Virgil furrowed his brow. "No, that can't be right. I don't faint."

"You fainted hard," Llewyn pointed out. He lowered the axe, setting the blade on the ground and leaning his massive forearms on the handle. "And fast, too. I don't mind telling you, that doesn't bode well for fighting supernatural evil."

"I didn't faint," Virgil insisted. "I took a strategic nap."

Simon snorted. "You are such a dope."

"Well, you shouldn't go swinging axes at people's throats anyway!" Virgil exploded, leveling an accusatory finger at the wizard's chest.

Llewyn stared down at him, amused. "Do you think that Dark Creatures will be any less aggressive?" he asked.

"Well...no," Virgil admitted, shrinking back. He rubbed his neck, enjoying the feeling of it, and the solid way it connected his head to his shoulders. "But I expect it from them."

"Expect it from everyone," Llewyn instructed. "You never know when a wolf might come at you dressed like a sheep."

"I don't think that's quite how the saying goes," Virgil said.

"But we get the point," Simon added quickly.

Virgil nodded his agreement. "Yeah. We do."

"At any rate, no matter *who* comes at you, your best defense is a strong defense." He scrutinized Virgil with his one good eye. "Not a collapsible offense."

"Easy for you to say," Virgil murmured.

"Okay. So how do we defend ourselves?"

Llewyn nodded his approval. He appreciated a student who could stay on track. "With the power of kinesthetic magic."

Virgil raised his hand, but didn't wait to be called on before speaking. "You said that yesterday. Kinisatic."

"Kinesthetic," the mage corrected him.

"Whatever. What is that?"

"Yeah," Simon added thoughtfully, tapping a finger against his cheek, "doesn't kinesthetic mean, like, active? *Physically* active?"

"This magic has *not* been physically active," Virgil pointed out. "Mostly I just stand here and don't move and make it happen."

"Yeah," Simon agreed, "I hate saying it, but Virgil's right."

Llewyn straightened his spine and stood tall, staring down at the two younger men. "A question I wasn't expecting for another several sessions," he admitted admiringly. "You two are a deep well of surprises." He picked up the axe and twirled it between his hands, spinning it as easily as if it were a pencil. "The magic you're tapping into *is* kinesthetic, even though it doesn't feel like it to you. Because even though you're standing still here, in our reality, the truth is, every time you dig down into your being and pull out your magic, another version of you, on a *different* plane of reality—and yes, I fully understand that you have a hard time believing in other planes of reality," he added quickly, looking mostly at Simon. "Despite that, there *is* another version of you, a you that shares all your *you-ness*, that exists on the dynagogical plane, and you're connected by an unbreakable bond. Every time you feel the power well up from the pit of your stomach, the other you is spinning and spinning and spinning, like a child's top, to generate a mystical power, and he sends it to you through the space-time link, filling your gut with the strength so you can tap into it there and move it into the other parts of your body, and out into the world. Your dynagogical other is like your generator, keeping you fueled... keeping you strong."

Simon furrowed his brow, and he blinked a few times. "There was never anything about a dynagogical generator-self in science class," he pointed out.

"Science only knows so much," Llewyn returned. "To understand the rest of reality, you need someone who can tap into its magic."

Virgil was also lost in deep thought, and he held up both of his hands and waved them through the air. "Wait, wait, wait," he said. "Does my dynamagical self—"

"Dynagogical," the wizard corrected him.

"Dynagogical, whatever—does he know that I exist?"

"Maybe someday you'll ask him." Llewyn turned his attention back to the axe. "You can use that magic to protect yourself from attacks. The process for putting up a shield is the same as the process for casting magic forward, like when you tried to hit the can. Except instead of shooting the energy forward, you spread it out before you. Eventually, you'll be able to do both at your whim, but for now, not wearing the manacle will make the shielding spell easier." He set the axe on the ground and resumed his normal, broad posture. He raised his hands, holding out his palms and spreading his fingers, as if he were holding someone—or something—at bay. His lips moved, and two flat planes of energy burst into existence, spreading out from his palms and extending like platters in front of his hands. They looked to be semi-solid, almost as if they were made from a translucent orange plastic that was filled with light. "Pick up the axe," Llewyn said.

Simon and Virgil looked at each other. "This sounds like a trick," Simon decided.

"Yeah, but I'm weirdly okay with it," Virgil replied. He reached down and lifted up the axe. It was heavy. *Extraordinarily* heavy. Even though Llewyn had held it easily with one hand, it took Virgil every ounce of strength he had in both of his arms to pick it up off the ground. He grunted with effort as he lifted it up to chest height. Within moments, he was covered in a flop sweat. "Now what?" he panted.

The wizard grinned. "Take my head off," he said.

Virgil snorted. The embarrassment of fainting was still fresh in his cheeks. "Gladly," he grunted. He used all his strength to heft the axe onto his shoulder. It pushed down on his bones like a hydraulic press. "Holy Hamburg, this thing is heavy," he muttered, shaking the beads of sweat from his forehead.

"I have a hatchet somewhere, if you'd prefer," the wizard said, smirking behind his orange shields. "In the toy box, in the nursery. For babies. Should I get it?"

Simon laughed out loud. "That was good," he admitted.

Virgil glowered. "I'm not a baby," he panted through gritted teeth.

He turned his torso, giving himself a bit of torque. Then he spun back around, letting the weight of the axe carry itself off of his shoulder with the centrifugal force, so that he only sort-of swung it without having to actually lift it any higher. The head of the axe turned sideways as Virgil heaved it through the air, and the broad side of it collided clumsily with the wizard's shields with a loud *CLANG*.

The shields held strong. The axe bounced off of them, vibrating so hard that Virgil's whole body trembled. He dropped the axe, and it fell to the floor with a thud. His breaths came heavy and hard. He put his hands on his hips and doubled over, trying to catch his breath. "Okay, I get it," he said, dismissing the wizard. "The shields are strong."

"*Very* strong," Llewyn confirmed. He closed his hands, and the orange light dissipated. "Strong enough to withstand attacks from almost any weapon that's manmade. It'll protect from most magics, too, if you can make it strong enough. It won't protect from everything…not the more powerful attacks from a demon like Asag, but it'll serve as a defense for some. It's a start, at any rate."

"Okay," Simon nodded, rubbing his hands together. "How do we do it?"

The wizard picked up the axe and gave it a practice swing. "Trial by fire," he grinned. Then he swung the axe again, this time at Simon.

And this time, the wizard didn't stop until he made contact.

CHAPTER 21

"I can't *believe* you stopped that first swing!" Virgil chirped excitedly as he clicked his seatbelt into place. "Man. *Man*. I was pretty angry about the whole fainting thing, but *man*. Seeing you just jump into action when he tried to cut you in half! *Man!*"

"I don't know what happened!" Simon replied excitedly, closing the car door behind him. "It was just pure instinct! He was like, *swing*! And I was like, *block*!"

"The way those shields just sprang from your hands! Amazing!"

"I know!" Simon cried. Even now, several hours later, exhausted and sore from their training session, he was still feeling the tingling excitement of having made his first kinesthetic shields.

"Even though the axe cracked through them, they were so good!"

"Yeah, I mean, did you see the *size* of that axe? For a first try, even though they cracked in half, *still*! That was *awesome*!" He gazed down at his hands and marveled at them. "I really am a wizard," he breathed.

"You're not a wizard," Llewyn said, appearing suddenly at the window. Simon and Virgil both screamed.

"Criminy, Llewyn!" Virgil said, placing a hand over his heart. "You scared us to death."

The sorcerer smirked. "You're not wizards," he said again. "You've got magic in you, all right. We'll make it strong. But you've got a long way to go before you're wizards. A long, long, *long* way."

"It was just a…figure of speech," Simon mumbled, looking down at the steering wheel, embarrassed.

"I need a favor," Llewyn said. "I tried to reach out to Abby just now, and I felt her energy, but it felt...wrong."

Simon frowned. "Wrong how?" he asked.

But the wizard shook his head. "Not sure, really. It felt like..." He twisted up his face, as if finding the right word was causing him discomfort. "I don't know, her energy felt like... *straw*."

Virgil blinked. "Straw?" he repeated. "Like...hay?"

Llewyn nodded. "Yeah. Doesn't make much sense, I know. But her energy has the feel of earthiness, and dust, and it's scratchy now."

"What does her energy normally feel like?" Simon asked.

Llewyn scratched his cheek. "Like milled cedar," he decided.

Simon considered this. "Huh," he said.

Llewyn knocked his hand against the roof of the car. "The fact that I can't reach her is...troubling. Find her."

"We will," Simon said, turning the keys in the ignition.

"Good." The wizard straightened up and stepped back toward the drainage ditch. "An energy shift that drastic...I don't know what it means, but I don't think it can be good."

CHAPTER 22

They stood inside the entrance to Squeezy Cheez and let their eyes adjust to the darkness. "I know I say this a lot," Simon said, looking around at all the children and the flashing lights, "but why do we keep coming here?"

"'Cause it's got the best animatronic band in town," Virgil answered, nodding toward the back room, where the huge, jerky robots were whirring to life. They were old, those robots, probably wrenched together sometime in the early 80s, but they somehow never seemed to look any worse from one year to the next. They certainly didn't look *good*; they were rusty, and their paint was flaking off, and sometimes their motors jerked their limbs too hard, and the robots would rock dangerously on their moorings. But in the ten years since Simon and Virgil had starting coming to Squeezy Cheez, the robots hadn't changed a bit.

They were oversized, anthropomorphic animals, most of them. Squeezy Cheez himself was a dog that looked like a cheap Goofy knock-off, with his floppy black ears and his long, pale snout. Suzie Kablooie was a female sheep with a long blonde ponytail. Her face was covered with splotches of pizza sauce, and her fur was blown backward, like she had just witnessed a terrible pizza-pie explosion. She played the electric guitar. Phony Pepperoni was the antagonist of the group; he was a duck with a pencil-thin mustache stuck to the end of his beak. He wore a boxy, pinstriped gangster suit, and there was a poorly-tilted fedora perched on his head, and he held a plastic saxophone in his hands. Pippa Pepper, the keyboard player, was a raccoon with green fur around her eyes instead of the traditional black, and the final member of the band, Crust Man, was, inexplicably, a huge piece of lightly-chewed pizza crust that had sprouted arms and legs.

"They really phoned in Crust Man," Virgil observed aloud, for maybe the thousandth time.

"I don't think they put a whole lot of thought into *any* of them," Simon said. Then he shivered.

The animatronics had always given him the creeps.

The game room was quiet, which wasn't surprising for dinnertime on a weeknight. Most of the families were gathered in the back room, sitting at the long community tables and watching the Squeezy Cheez band with reactions ranging from exquisite delight to absolute fear.

A few stragglers had gathered near the new race car videogame, and some scrawny kid with Coke-bottle glasses was hitting every single basket on the Pop-A-Shot, but otherwise, they had the game room to themselves.

"There's Abby," Virgil said, lifting his chin toward the line of pinball games. Abby was bent over the glass of the Ninja Frogs machine, wiping the glass with an old, mottled rag.

They crossed the room, Simon's heart swelling a bit as they got closer. He was all the way gone where Abby was concerned. There wasn't much use denying it.

He had a crush.

"Hey, Abby," he said as they approached.

She didn't look up. She just kept wiping the glass.

"Now *that* is some serious dedication to grade school gunk," Virgil teased, watching her scrub at some sticky residue left behind by one of the children from the day.

Still, Abby didn't respond. She kept her head down and worked the rag over the glass.

Simon frowned. "Abby?" he asked. He stepped up to the other side of the pinball machine and placed his hands on the edge. He leaned down, trying to see her eyes. "Abby?"

She didn't look up. She just cleaned the glass.

"Hey! Abs!" Virgil clapped his hands to try to get her attention. She didn't even flinch. Instead, she finished with the spot of residue, picked up her rag, picked up the spray bottle of cleaner, and moved on to the next pinball machine.

Simon and Virgil exchanged confused looks.

"Energy like straw," Virgil said.

"It's definitely not blueberry," Simon replied.

They hurried over to the next pinball machine, and Virgil waved his hand in front of Abby's downturned eyes. "Hello? Abby?"

She didn't register them. She just sprayed the cleaning solution and started to wipe at the glass.

"Abby..." Simon said, reaching out and touching her shoulder. She flinched then, and pulled back, turning away from the pinball machine. She raised the spray bottle and squirted a mist of vinegar and water into Simon's eyes.

"Owww!" he cried, stumbling backward blindly and throwing his hands over his eyes. His whole face burned, and tears immediately sprang up in his eyes, flushing out the vinegar. "What is *that* about?" he cried, keeping his eyes shut.

He felt Virgil's hand on his arm. "Come on," Virgil murmured, pulling him away. "Let's go talk over there. This is all wrong."

"Oh, you think?!" Simon demanded, scrubbing at his eyes. He blinked them open, and the flashing arcade lights felt like powerful lasers against his vision. He closed his eyes again. "What did she do *that* for?"

"Something is seriously wrong here," Virgil said, leading him back toward the front counter.

"No kidding," Simon snapped. The burn in his eyes was subsiding. He opened them again, and the world came into a watery focus. "What do you think is going on?" he asked.

Virgil shrugged. "No idea. It's almost like she's under some sort of spell."

Simon started. "What if she *is* under some kind of spell?"

"Yeah, but...how? I mean, unless some dark magic got into her apartment last night. You and I were with her until late, and we all left Mrs. Grunberg's house at the same time. She's working a double today, right? So she's been here since they opened at ten. That's not a huge window for the Forces of Evil to work their magic on her brain." He looked back over at Abby, who had moved on to a third pinball machine. "Still...I mean, I totally understand being put off by your advances, but cleaning spray to the eyes is a little harsh."

"But that's just it; she's *not* put off by my..." He stopped himself, then waved his hands through the air. "Not *advances*...I'm not making *advances*. I'm not a creeper."

"Says you," Virgil said.

"Shut up. They're not advances. But, like...she touched my arm last night when we said goodbye. And I know," he said quickly, because Virgil had opened his mouth to speak, "I know that's not, like, a declaration of love or anything, but it's also definitely not a 'don't ever touch me or I'll spray vinegar in your eyes' kind of move, either."

Virgil rubbed his chin. "Hm. Yeah. That's true."

"Do you think this is Asag?" Simon asked, looking over Virgil's shoulder and watching Abby carefully. "Or something else?"

"I don't know," Virgil admitted, turning to follow Simon's gaze. "We know there's a lot of weird stuff that happens in Templar. I wouldn't be surprised at all if it was something that didn't have anything to do with Asag."

"Neither would I." Simon frowned as he watched Abby finish with the pinball machines and walk over toward the Whac-

A-Mole game. She moved with a strange stiffness; her spine was completely straight, and her arms and legs moved as if they were on pistons. "Still...something about this feels...related."

"Yeah," Virgil sighed. "Yeah, it does."

Abby mindlessly scrubbed at the surface of the Whac-A-Mole, spraying the cleaner and wiping it away with a completely blank expression on her face.

"So what do we do?" Virgil asked.

Simon shook his head. "I have no idea."

In the next room, the animatronic Squeezy Cheez band finished up their set. The robots bowed clumsily at the waist, all of them ratcheting down too hard, and too fast, and bobbing precariously at the bottoms of their bows. Then they reared back up, blinked their eyes, and moved along their tracks, crossing back to the rear end of the stage. The shiny purple curtain pulled itself closed across the back of the stage, hiding all of the robots. As it passed them, Squeezy Cheez gave his usual final goodbye: "Thank you, everybody! You guys are on *fire!*"

The lighting in the dining area changed, becoming brighter for the patrons. They began to chatter to each other, and Simon turned to Virgil, blocking them out of his mind. "Am I wrong to think this might call for something drastic?" he asked.

Virgil eyed him suspiciously. "I guess I would say that depends on how drastic you're talking."

"Pretty drastic," Simon replied. "Call me crazy, but the Squeezy Cheez band just gave me an idea."

"If the Squeezy Cheez band gave you an idea, then you *are* crazy," Virgil pointed out.

Simon strode over to the unmanned game room counter, and he pushed his way through the swinging door marked "Employees Only."

"Simon!" Virgil gasped. "That's against the rules!"

Simon ignored him. He crossed behind the counter until he found the trash can near the register. He picked it up and set it on the counter. It was filled with paper receipts and candy wrappers, mostly. Then Simon turned to the wire shelves on the wall behind him, the ones that held all the prizes people exchanged their tickets for. One of the bins was filled with cheap metal lighters. Simon pulled one out, flicked it open, and struck his thumb against the wheel. A flame instantly sparked to life, waving like a serpent caught in some flute-player's spell.

"Are you about to do what I think you're about to do?" Virgil asked, his eyes wide.

"It's totally safe," Simon protested. "Trash cans are, like, made for this."

He lowered the flame down into the trash can. The papers caught almost instantly, springing to life in a flickering fire.

"Fire!" the kid playing Pop-A-Shot cried, pointing at the trash can and shrieking. "Fire!"

The call was picked up instantly by the parents in the second room, and they all sprang into action, gathering up their children and pulling them toward the exit. They all ran toward the door, and one of the mothers pulled the fire alarm handle on her way out. A siren immediately began to blare, and fire sprinklers popped down from the ceiling, showering the entire establishment. Soon, the only people who were left inside Squeezy Cheez were Simon, Virgil, and Abby.

The fire in the trash can began to flicker out, its flames dying against the downpour of water.

"Oh," Virgil said, spitting water off of his lips. "*That's* what you meant by 'drastic.'"

"And it was drastic, as promised," Simon replied, not taking his eyes off of Abby. He nodded in her direction. "But look."

Virgil turned his head to get a better view. Abby was still

bent over the Whac-A-Mole game, running her rag over the increasingly wet surface. Her hair hung down over her eyes in wet, purple tendrils, and her glasses were too splattered with water for her to see through.

"Okay, this is too weird," Virgil decided. He pushed the water back off of his own hair. "She's like a robot." His eyes grew wide. "Oh man...do you think Abby's actually a robot?"

Simon shook his head. "No way. If she were a robot, she'd short-circuit in the water."

"Oh," Virgil said. "True."

Simon moved out from behind the counter and walked cautiously toward Abby. "One more thing to try," he said.

"What?" Virgil asked, coming up close behind him.

"She's a strong empath, right? She feels other people's memories with skin-to-skin contact. So if I touch her, that should give her something to react to."

"But she's wearing her gloves," Virgil noted. "They cover her arms up to her sleeves."

"Then I'll touch her ear," Simon replied, growing frustrated.

"Dude. You don't go around touching other people's ears. That's weird."

"Is it less weird to touch her face?" Simon demanded.

Virgil thought about that. "Well, yeah, kind of," he decided.

"Virgil. I'm going to touch her in an appropriate place for a very short amount of time and see if she responds, or if she's under some sort of numbing spell or something. Okay?"

"She *did* react pretty strongly when she touched you bare-handed the other day," Virgil recalled. He nodded. "Okay. Do it."

"I'm *going* to do it, that's why I told you that's what I'm doing," Simon pointed out. "Stop trying to steal credit for my ideas."

He crept up closer. Abby didn't notice them; she just kept cleaning the Whac-A-Mole machine. The sleeves of her denim jacket were pushed up around her elbows, her arms bare from her forearm down to her fingertips. Simon walked up behind her, took a deep breath, reached out, and touched her ear.

Nothing happened. Abby didn't so much as flinch.

"All right, enough of this," Virgil said. He strode up and clapped his hands right in front of her eyes. Abby didn't even look up. Virgil shook out his arms, then he closed his eyes. He stretched out his hands. He focused on the energy magic in his gut, and he pushed it out through his arms. His fingertips glowed with orange light.

"What're you doing?" Simon hissed, giving Virgil a shove. "You can't magic-shoot her!"

"I *have* to magic-shoot her, look at her, Simon, she's a total automaton!"

"She's still a person, Virgil, you'll kill her! You don't have a manacle to control it! And even *with* the manacle, you're a terrible shot!"

"Well I don't see as how we have any choice! She doesn't respond to movement, or sound, or to empathy! We have to snap her out of it!"

"This isn't going to snap her out of it," Simon cried, snatching up one of Virgil's glowing hands, "it's going to melt her!"

"It's not going to *melt* her, don't be so dramatic! We just need to give her a little fire-jolt jumpstart. Haven't you ever seen *Temple of Doom*?"

"Of course I've seen *Temple of Doom*, how is this anything like that?" Simon demanded.

"Indy gets taken over by the evil cannibal spirit, and Short Round has to bring him back to himself. It is *just* like this!"

Simon rubbed his chin. "You are so stupid," he said, shaking his head. Then he thought about it for a second. "But yeah, I guess that *is* sort of like this…"

"Exactly." Virgil crossed his arms in triumph. "And how did Short Round bring Indy out of it?"

Simon sighed. "He set him on fire with a torch."

"*He set him on fire with a torch*. Exactly." He uncrossed his arms and held up one hand. It lit up from within, radiating its orange light. "So I'm going to burn Abby, *very lightly*, and she's going to wake up, too."

Simon bit his bottom lip nervously. He looked at Abby. "Fine," he sighed, putting up his hands and stepping back. "But I swear, if you do any permanent damage…"

"I'm not going to do any permanent damage, I'm a professional."

"No, you're not."

Virgil stepped around the Whac-A-Mole machine, his hands glowing with bright magic. Abby reached out for the spray bottle, and as she did, Virgil reached down toward her fingers. The light from his hands seemed to extend from his skin, reaching toward Abby's hand.

Suddenly, Abby looked up. She seemed to register Virgil for the first time. She snatched her hand back, as if she had been close to touching a flame. She glared at Virgil, her eyes burning with anger, and she reached out toward him. Virgil was startled, and he stumbled backward, out of harm's way, but as Abby stretched forward, her arms seemed to unravel from her shoulders, and like an unspooling thread, they swirled and became thinner and thinner, and longer and longer, reaching for him. Virgil cried out as he backed into the Pop-A-Shot. With his back against the game cabinet, he tried to dart to his left, but Abby's long, tangled arm slammed up against the cabinet just past his shoulder. Virgil stopped, then tried to spin around the other way, but Abby's other hand burst past him on that side, too. He was trapped.

Simon gaped at the sight before him. Virgil was pinned into place against the Pop-A-Shot by Abby's outstretched arms, even though Abby herself was still standing behind the Whac-A-Mole game, at least ten feet away from Virgil. Her arms hung loosely from her shoulders like Slinkys, drooping down in the middle and inclining back up to meet her hands. The sleeves of her denim jacket only stretched so far; they had started at her elbows, but now they only covered the upper parts of her biceps. The rest of her arms, stretched out to seven or eight times their normal lengths, were thin and fraying, like threads.

Simon's jaw fell open. He blinked hard. But when he opened his eyes, the scene before him hadn't changed. "Abby?" he said.

She turned her head. Her eyes were full of fury, and her cheeks were red with anger. The skin over her cheekbones began to peel back, bursting like blisters, as if her whole skin was stretched so thin that it was breaking away in other places. "*Discedite*," she hissed in a language that didn't sound like English, in a voice that didn't sound like her own. Then her eyes glowed with bright, white light, and she said it again, screaming it this time, so loud that Simon had to clamp his hands over his ears: "*DISCEDITE!*"

The windows of Squeezy Cheez exploded at the sound of her screech, and so did the glass from the display counters, and the glass on top of the pinball machine. From every direction, Simon heard the ear-shattering sound of glass popping and breaking. He covered his head with his arms and shrank back, crouching down behind a table, holding in place as the shards of glass fell around him like sleet.

When the glass stopped falling, he peeked through his arms. The lights had blown out, too, both the overhead lights and the neon lights. The water still sprayed from the fire sprinklers overhead, but they sprayed down into darkness now. The only light in the room came from the emergency lights near the exits, and from the glow of the overhead lights in the parking lot outside streaming through the windows. In the dimness, Simon looked up and saw Virgil, his eyes closed, his back pressed against the Pop-A-Shot cabinet. He stood there on trembling legs, not daring to open his eyes, and not daring to move.

But the hands on either side of his shoulders were gone. The arms that connected those hands to Abby's shoulders were gone.

Abby had disappeared.

Simon stood up carefully, turning his head, wiping the water out of his eyes, and scanning the restaurant for signs of life. But he and Virgil were alone.

"Virg? You okay?" Simon brushed some tiny flakes of glass off his shoulder and stepped toward the Pop-A-Shot. "Virg?"

Virgil slowly, carefully, opened his eyes. He exhaled with relief when he saw that Abby— and her unnaturally long arms—had disappeared. "Simon. What happened?"

"I don't know," Simon said, crossing the room, "but..."

He stopped short in his sentence. He looked down at the floor, just past the tips of his shoes.

Abby hadn't disappeared after all. She had just unraveled into a big heap of string.

Simon stooped down and stared, open-mouthed, and the pile of threads near his feet. Most of the threads were the pale-tan color of Abby's skin, and some were the stonewashed blue color of her denim jacket and jeans. A handful had been her purple hair, and a few wisps of brown had been her eyebrows, he guessed. He reached down and plunged his hands into the threads and lifted them up in front of his eyes.

They were just string. Cold, wet, lifeless string.

Simon held them up to Virgil. "Look," he said. His brain didn't seem capable of forming any words more complex than that.

Virgil tilted his head in confusion. He pushed himself off the Pop-A-Shot cabinet and walked over to where Simon was crouched on the floor. He peered down at the threads in Simon's hands. "Is that...yarn?" he asked, confused.

Simon nodded, his whole body moving slowly with disbelief. "It's Abby," he said.

Virgil screwed up his face in confusion. "But, like...that's not *really* Abby," he said, sounding uncertain. "Right?"

Simon blinked. "What are you asking me right now?"

"I'm asking you, is that *actually* Abby? Is Abby *actually* yarn?!"

Simon tossed the threads down onto the floor and stood up. "No, Virgil, I don't think Abby is actually yarn. I think this is a thing that was made of yarn that was made to *look* like Abby, and to *act* like Abby, sort of, though it wasn't very good at it. I think this is a fake Abby, and that would explain why Llewyn was getting such a weird energy from her today. Or...from *it*." He placed his hands on either side of his head, as if trying to keep his brain from escaping his skull. "I think someone has kidnapped Abby, and they tried to replace her with a doll."

Virgil's face flushed white. "Who would even have the ability to *do* that?" he asked.

Simon snorted. "Gee, Virgil, I don't know. In the last week, we've basically met two people who have the power to pull that kind of thing off. One of them is Llewyn, but he seems pretty solidly on our side, so I don't think it's him."

"He's kind of grumpy," Virgil pointed out.

"But he's also one of the good guys," Simon said, exasperated. "Besides, Abby introduced us to him, she trusts him. And we were with him all day today. It wasn't him. So who's the only other person we know with the kind of power to animate an Abby doll that's so lifelike, it fools everyone for almost an entire day?"

"Should I assume that you're not referring to the barista at the coffee shop this morning?"

Simon exhaled. "No. I am not."

"Right, I thought not. So. Asag, then."

Simon nodded. "Asag."

They both stared down at the mess of threads on the floor. "You think he has her?"

"Yeah. I do."

Virgil rubbed his face with his hands. The sprinklers stopped spraying water, and he and Simon took a few breaths of the dry, silent air. "When would he have gotten her, though? It doesn't seem like he leaves the basement. I mean, best as I can tell. And Abby went home last night when we did, and I doubt she was back out at the house this morning before work."

Simon inhaled sharply. His spine stiffened. "She probably didn't go back this morning," he said quietly, almost to himself. "But we don't know that she left when we did, either."

Virgil furrowed his brow. "What do you mean?"

"I mean, she walked us to my car, she said she was going home, we said goodnight...but we didn't actually see her get in her truck. We didn't see her drive away."

Virgil's eyes grew wide with understanding. "You think she stayed after we left?" He reached out and grabbed Simon's arm. "Do you think she went into the basement?"

"I wouldn't put it past her. Would you?"

Virgil's heart sank. "No. She seemed *super* intent on going inside."

"Exactly." Simon closed his eyes, pinched his temples, and cursed. "We have to get her out of there."

"Okay, it's not that I disagree, 'cause I don't, but I just want to say, you know that means facing the demon, right?"

"Yeah, I know," Simon said, shrugging off his friend and pacing around the room. "I know that."

"And again, not that I don't want to save Abby, but Llewyn said—"

"Llewyn won't leave his tent and use his extraordinary power to save the world!" Simon exploded. "I get it, I get that he can't, I get that he's focused on the thing that's burrowing toward his heart, I get it, fine. But he can't be out here, but we—we are *out here*, we are *in it*, and we have the power to do something, and we can't just sit around, waiting for the next six months while we get trained on how to throw knives and block spells or whatever."

"You think he's going to teach us how to throw knives?" Virgil asked, genuinely interested.

"Not the point! Look! I know what Llewyn said, and I know we're not ready, but I also know we surprised the demon last time with our protection spell, and that was before we knew anything about the magic that we've been practicing over the last two days, and shooting beams and throwing up shields and hiding Skee-Balls in psychic vaults, all that has to count for *something*! And Abby is down there, and she needs our help. I'm not going to just sit by while some old wizard draws out our training for the next eighty years, okay?"

Virgil frowned. His eyes looked pained. "You're saying all this like I might disagree with you, but...of *course* I want to use magic to try to bring down a demon. Man, do you know me at *all*? Of *course* I want to do that. And also, Abby seems super cool. You know I'm in. I mean, Llewyn's not going to like it. And we don't have our manacles."

Simon set his jaw. "It doesn't matter. We have to go save Abby."

Virgil grinned. "Those manacles feel more like bumper lanes anyway," he said. "My power needs to roam free and unleashed."

"Your power's going to get us all killed," Simon pointed out. "But maybe it'll kill the demon in the process."

"That's the spirit!" Virgil clapped his hand happily on Simon's back, and together, the pair of them crunched through the glass and the darkness toward the doors of the Squeezy Cheez.

"This is a stupid idea, isn't it?" Simon asked as he pushed open the front door.

"Oh, definitely," Virgil agreed. "But sometimes, being stupid is what it takes to be a hero of Templar."

CHAPTER 23

"Well. Here we are again."

They sat out in the Pontiac, across the street from Mrs. Grunberg's house. It was pretty much the same as they'd left it: dark windows above, pulsing red lights below. The flowers were still thick with inky shadows, and the splotch of it seemed to have reached the walkway that went around the side of the house, leading to the backyard. There were a couple of dim lights on in the upstairs windows—lamps, probably. But for the most part, the house was dark.

"Look," Simon said, nudging Virgil and pointing down the street. They could just make out the shape of Abby's truck.

It was in the same spot she'd parked it in the night before.

"Guess that answers that question," Virgil said.

Simon nodded. "And it looks like someone's home," he said, nodding up at the light coming from the upstairs window.

"Yeah, but barely. Geez, do you think they know they can turn more lights on? Like, enough to actually see?"

"Sometimes old people go to bed early," Simon shrugged.

"How early? It's not even 9:00. And what about her grandson? Shouldn't he be watching the CW or something in the living room?"

"Maybe he's out," Simon murmured. He opened the door and stepped out into the street. "And it doesn't matter. We're not going upstairs." He stared at the red light coming through the basement windows, and he shivered. "Abby's in the basement."

Virgil got out of the car and joined his friend in the street. They crossed over to the Mrs. Grunberg's yard. "Are you sure you want to do this?"

"No," Simon said. "You?"

"Nope."

"Great. Then I guess we're doing it."

"I guess we are."

They crept along the edge of the property, trying to stay in the shadows. They passed the tree where they'd crouched with Abby the night before. Simon could still see the depressions they'd left in the soft dirt.

They made it as far as the walkway when they heard a voice from above them say, "Hey. What're you doing?"

They both froze. Simon looked up at the front porch. Mrs. Grunberg's grandson stood near the railing, looking down at them with a mixture of fear and confusion. He looked somehow worse than he had the night before. The dark circles under his eyes were darker and wider. His skin was so pale, they could practically see through it. His hair was mussed, and his clothes were baggy and disheveled.

"Oh. Uh…" Virgil began.

"Yeah, we're just…" Simon tried. But neither of them had come prepared with a lie.

The redheaded boy motioned them over. "Come inside." Then he turned around and went in through the front door.

"Geez, that kid gives me the creeps," Virgil shuddered. "What do we do?"

Simon sighed. "We can't exactly break into the basement if he knows we're here. So I guess we go up."

They circled back around and climbed the rickety wooden stairs to the front porch. They had never actually been inside Mrs. Grunberg's house before. Simon went first, easing the door open gently and peeking his head in. It was dark inside, with the rooms lit only sparingly by low lamps and candles. The front door opened up into a stairwell that led to the second floor.

There were two separate room areas flanking the staircase, a dining room and a parlor. The dining room looked like it hadn't been touched in decades; the big wooden table was draped with a dusty white sheet, and the six chairs that were stationed around the table had been likewise covered with cloth. An antique buffet stood in the corner, but the glass panes set into its doors were so covered with dust and grime that Simon couldn't see through them enough to even tell if there were dishes stacked inside.

The parlor on the right looked slightly more welcoming. The furniture was uncovered and looked well-used. The loveseat and the armchair were old, antique pieces, with wooden scrollwork at the feet and arms, and with torn upholstery, the colors of which had faded with time. A low coffee table between the couches was set with a short candelabra, and all five of the candles were lit.

The grandson moved quickly and silently through the parlor, disappearing into the next room like a ghost.

"Man, I knew her house would be haunted," Virgil said, inspecting the dark rooms, "but this is ridiculous."

"It's not haunted...it's just old," Simon whispered. But he didn't know if he was convinced of that himself.

The followed the grandson into a kitchen, which looked to be slightly updated compared to the rest of the house, but not by much. The Formica table and off-white appliances with their rusty knobs gave the room a distinct 1960s feel. An old coffee percolator sat atop the lit stove. The grandson pulled it off the flame. "Coffee?" he asked, pouring himself a cup.

"No, thank you," Virgil said quickly.

"It's a little late for coffee, isn't it?" Simon asked.

"I don't sleep much," the boy answered quietly. He blew the steam away from his mug and stared into nothingness as he took a sip.

"Maybe you should stop drinking so much coffee," Virgil suggested. Simon elbowed him. "Ow."

But the grandson didn't seem to hear him. "I'm Neil," he said, by way of introduction, though he didn't extend a hand to shake. He just sipped again from his coffee.

"Oh. Uh...I'm Simon. And this is Virgil. We're friends of your grandma."

Virgil cleared his throat. "We're not *friends* of hers," he clarified. "We know her, but we don't, like, go bowling together or anything."

"Grandma is in the sleeping room," Neil said, holding the coffee cup under his chin.

Simon and Virgil exchanged uneasy looks. "We usually call that the bedroom," Virgil said, trying to break the tension.

"Would you like to see her?" Neil asked, staring at the floor.

About a million different alarm bells were ringing in Simon's head. "Uh, no. I think we're good," he said. He grabbed Virgil by the elbow and pulled him out of the kitchen, back into the parlor. "Geez, this kid is *seriously* gone," he whispered.

"Oh, you think?" Virgil hissed back.

"He's totally sleep-deprived. That can lead to some serious insanity."

"I know, I've seen *Insomnia*."

"That movie's really good."

"I know."

"Anyway," Simon continued, glancing over his shoulder to see if Neil was listening to them. He wasn't. "The poor kid's out of his mind. We have to get rid of the demon downstairs. Like, not just save Abby, but banish Asag, too."

"Well, no kidding. What did you think we were going to do, go down and ask the demon to let Abby go, and then slip out the backdoor when he wasn't looking?" Virgil shot back.

"I don't know what I thought," Simon answered honestly. "I'm making this up as I go along."

"That must be why it's going so well," Virgil whispered, rolling his eyes.

"Let's tell the kid we're leaving, then circle around and get downstairs," Simon suggested.

"Yeah," Virgil said seriously, "if I'm gonna die tonight, I'd rather get it over with."

They turned back toward the kitchen, and Neil was standing right next to them. They both screamed. "Holy Hamburg! Neil! You can't just sneak up on people like that," Virgil said.

"Do you want to see the sleeping room?" Neil asked. He covered his mouth as he let loose a yawn.

"No, we actually...sort of have to go," Simon said. "We'll take the tour next time." He pushed Virgil back through the parlor, and they hurried to the front door. Simon reached down and turned the handle.

It was locked.

"Did you lock the door?" he asked, annoyed. He reached down to unlock it, but was surprised to see there was no lock to turn. There was only a keyhole.

"I didn't lock it," Virgil said.

Simon exhaled. His heart dropped into the pit of his stomach. He ran his fingers over the keyhole. "No." He turned back to Neil, who had followed them through the parlor. "He did."

"What?" Virgil asked. "How...?"

Neil pulled a key from his pocket and held it tightly in one pale fist. "We have to see the sleeping room," he said. Then he turned and moved up the stairs, slowly ascending to the second floor.

"This is bad," Virgil said, watching the redheaded boy climb the stairs. "Bad, bad, bad, bad, bad."

"Asag is really doing a number on him," Simon said, trying to keep the fear out of his voice.

"What do we do?"

Simon swallowed hard. "I guess we go up."

"Simon, I don't—"

"Don't worry," Simon said, working hard to sound confident. "I have a plan." Then he added, "Sort of." He began to climb the stairs.

"Oh, great. A sort-of plan." Virgil sighed, but he followed them up the steps.

Neil was waiting for them on the landing. The upstairs hallway was lit only by a single sconce on the wall, and it threw long shadows down the dark passageway. Neil's eyes were hidden by the shadow of his brow, and the dark circles beneath them served to give him the look of a man with black holes for eye sockets. "Are you ready to go to the sleeping room?" he asked.

"Uh, not quite," Simon said. "Could we use the bathroom first?"

"We?" Virgil asked, raising an eyebrow.

Simon ignored him.

Neil frowned. "I have to ask," he said slowly. Simon was about to inquire after who, exactly, Neil needed to ask, when the younger boy turned away and began whispering into his own hands. After a few seconds, he turned back and said, "You can use it."

"Great," Simon said. "Where is it?"

Neil raised a hand and pointed into the darkness of the hallway, toward the back of the house. "There," was all he said.

"Cool. Got it. Thanks." Simon grabbed Virgil by the collar and dragged him quickly down the hallway, into the darkness.

"Hey!" Virgil protested. But he let himself be pulled along.

They found the bathroom at the end of the hall, and Simon flipped on the light switch inside. The light was a sickly blue that reminded Virgil of a hospital room. He looked back down the hallway and saw Neil watching them.

As Simon closed the door, Virgil could swear he saw a second human-shaped shadow spread out on the wooden floor next to Neil's, even though no one was standing there.

Then the door was closed, Virgil snapped back to his senses.

"*Man*, that kid is creepy," he said. "Also, I know we're friends, so don't take this the wrong way, but I'd really prefer it if you handled going to the bathroom on your own."

"I'm not going to the bathroom...we're getting out of here." Simon crossed the small room and stepped up onto the closed toilet seat. There was a small window set into the wall over the tank, a window that looked out over the backyard. Simon opened the window and was relieved to find there was no window screen. He poked his head outside and studied the ground below. "I think we can make it," he decided.

"Are you crazy? We're in the second story!" Virgil cried.

"There's a metal awning over the kitchen window below. I think I can lower myself down onto that, then hop down to the ground." He pulled his head back inside and turned around, throwing one leg out the window. "Give me a hand."

"This is so, so stupid," Virgil grumbled, but he stepped forward and took Simon's hand.

Simon kicked his other leg out the window and sat on the sill. "This is going to work out great," he said, nodding enthusiastically.

"Five bucks says it doesn't," Virgil replied.

"You're on." Simon spun over in the window so his belly was pressing against the sill. Virgil gripped his friend's arm with both of his own hands, and he lowered Simon down the side of the house. He heard Simon's sneakers scuff against the metal of the awning, and then the weight of his arms went slack. "I'm good!" Simon called up, and Virgil let go. He peeked out the window and saw Simon hop down from the awning and into the soft grass below.

Simon turned back up and motioned at his friend. "Your turn!"

"Who's going to help *me* down?!" Virgil demanded. But Simon just glanced nervously around the backyard, then made impatient arm motions up at Virgil. He grumbled and turned around, sticking one foot out the window.

Virgil pushed himself out, holding onto the windowsill with every ounce of strength he could summon. He gripped it so hard, his fingers turned white. He eased his feet down, swinging them blindly, trying to feel for the metal awning. He hung there for a few seconds, like a cat on a screen door, until finally his toes scraped against metal. He exhaled a sigh of relief. He let go of the sill and dropped down...but he had only found the edge of the awning, and his foot slipped off of it, and he went tumbling down the side of the house. He hit the ground hard and collapsed in a heap.

"Ow," he said weakly.

Simon frowned down at his friend. "That's not how you're supposed to do that," he said. He reached down and helped Virgil to his feet. "You okay?"

"I'm invincible," Virgil replied weakly. He swooned, and Simon caught him.

"Yeah. Pretty invincible."

"Look, can we just go fight the demon now?" Virgil asked, steadying himself.

Simon opened his mouth to respond, but just then, the basement door blew open from the inside, slamming against the wall, making them both jump. Dense mist roiled up from the basement steps, spilling out into the yard, tinged blood-red by the flashing light radiating from below.

"Guess we didn't catch him by surprise," Simon said.

Virgil looked Simon in the eye and clapped him on the shoulder. "We can do this," he said seriously. "We've been training."

"For two whole days."

"That's more than we had the first time."

"Good point." Simon looked at the open door and took a deep breath. "Okay," he said finally, shaking out his hands and bouncing from one foot to the other. "For Abby. And for Neil. Let's go send Asag back to hell."

CHAPTER 24

They stood at the opening to the basement and peered into the blowing red fog. "Why is it foggy?" Virgil asked.

"I don't know," Simon shrugged. "For effect?"

The haze clung close to the steps; when it reached the top of the stairs, it spread out across the ground like a blanket. It was so thick that Simon and Virgil couldn't see their sneakers.

"If I lift up my leg, and I don't have a foot anymore because this hell-fog has eaten through my shoes and dissolved it away, I swear…" Virgil held his breath and picked up his knee.

His shoe was still intact.

"Phew."

"We should have brought the candle," Simon said, kicking himself for being so thoughtless. "The one spell that worked, and we didn't bring the candle that we need to do it."

Virgil tilted his head thoughtfully. "Do you think this would work?" He reached into his pocket and pulled out a lighter.

"Why do you have a lighter?" Simon asked suspiciously.

"I swiped it from Squeezy Cheez."

"That's stealing," Simon pointed out.

"Oh, come on…*that's* what's bothering you? The fact that I took a lighter after a yarn-dummy tried to murder me and then exploded all the glass out of the windows? What you should really be concerned about is why on earth a place like Squeezy Cheez offers lighters as a prize to kids."

"Huh. Yeah, that *is* pretty strange," Simon admitted.

"Do you think it'll work?"

"Instead of a candle? I don't know," Simon said doubtfully. "Worth a try, I guess. You still have that spell on your phone?"

Virgil pulled out his phone and tapped on the screen. A few seconds later, he had brought up the protection spell. "Bingo," he said proudly.

"Great." Simon swiped the phone and cleared his throat. Virgil flicked the lighter to life, and Simon stumbled through the words a second time. When he reached the end of the spell, the flame of the lighter exploded into the giant fist of fire. Virgil cried out in pain as the flames, now comically oversized against the tiny metal lighter, licked at his fingers. The flame spun through its color wheel, yellow to orange to blue to red to green to purple, and then it settled back into its regular size, flickering with its blueish-purple fire.

"Well, I didn't enjoy that," Virgil said miserably. He checked his arm for burns, but he appeared to be okay.

"But it worked," Simon said, nodding at the flame.

Virgil frowned down at the lighter. "How are we both supposed to hold this thing?" It was a good question; even holding it by just his fingers, the lighter was completely swallowed up by his comparatively large size.

"I guess we don't," Simon said. "I'll walk behind you. Just...don't break away. Don't leave me uncovered."

Virgil nodded. "Got it."

They stepped cautiously into the stairwell, Virgil leading the way, and Simon crouching close behind him. They eased down the staircase, feeling for the next step down with their toes. The mist continued to roil up past them. When they reached the bottom of the stairs, the door above slammed shut behind them, and they both jumped and screamed.

"*Why* was I not ready for that?" Virgil said, trying to regain control of his breath.

Simon was about to respond, but another voice filled the gloomy red basement then:

"My young disciples have returned."

As their eyes adjusted to the darkness, they could see the familiar sight of Asag, sitting in his chair. He was still wearing the same suit, and he still had the baby mask fitted over his face.

They couldn't see beyond him, though, to the far end of the basement; the sourceless, pulsing red light made it impossible for their eyes to adjust to the darkness of the far end of the room.

"Disciples?" Virgil said, his voice trembling. He was trying his best to sound even, and fearless, but it wasn't quite working. "We didn't come here to follow you; we came here to destroy you."

"Hm." Asag seemed to be considering this seriously. He noted the purple flame dancing on top of the lighter. "Is that true, Simon?" he asked, tilting his head.

It was creepy, watching the expressionless mask turn to the side like that.

"Of course," Simon said, forcing himself to speak.

"You didn't come here because you couldn't resist our reunion?" the demon asked, sounding honestly intrigued.

Simon squinted in confusion, peering at Asag over Virgil's shoulder. "Our reunion?" he asked. "What are you talking about?"

The demon sighed. He leaned back in his wooden chair and crossed his legs. "I've been calling you. Haven't you felt it? Haven't you *seen* it?"

Simon thought back to the strange flashes of Asag he had seen...first out at Llewyn's tent, then again last night, out in Mrs. Grunberg's front yard. "No," he lied, but he could hear his own voice falter. "I didn't see anything."

Asag clicked his tongue, sounding his disapproval. "Now, Simon, don't lie to me. I serve the Lord of Lies. I can pick a lie out of the air as if it were a speck of dust floating lazily by."

He brushed a piece of lint from the shoulder of his suit. "We have a connection, you and I. You've seen my true face. That's not something many people can say." He chuckled quietly to himself. The he slapped his palms down on both of his knees, uncrossed his legs, and stood up from the chair. "Well, you've piqued my interest. If you're not here to serve me, boys, why *have* you come?"

"We're here for Abby," Simon said, taking a step out from behind Virgil, and away from the protection spell. He realized his mistake almost instantly, and he hopped back into place, peeking out over Virgil's shoulder. "Let her go, and we'll think about letting you live."

Virgil turned and looked at Simon with surprise. "Dude. Nice," he said admiringly.

The demon began to walk...but, Virgil noticed, not toward them. The protection spell seemed to be working. He decided to try their luck, and he took two steps forward, following Asag toward the front of the basement.

"Abby?" the demon asked. "Poor Simon, I think you're confused."

"I think you're a liar," Simon spat. He grabbed Virgil's shoulders and began to steer him toward the back of the basement, walking with the flame facing Asag so that they were stepping carefully back into the darkness.

"When I have to be," Asag admitted. He ran a scaly hand over his bald scalp. The porcelain mask shifted on his face. "But I find it would give me no advantage at present."

"You have her," Simon shot back confidently. "We're setting her free and taking her home."

"Hm. And I have her chained up in the back, is that it?" Asag asked, his voice curious.

"Of course you do," Simon growled. He and Virgil continued to step backward, away from the demon, into the darkness. The purple lighter flame provided little light, and they each had the sense of being swallowed by a giant mouth.

"Poor Simon," the demon said, his voice now bright with glee. "What *will* you do when you reach that back wall and find that it's only the three of us down here?"

Virgil turned and looked over his shoulder. "Simon...?" he asked nervously.

"He's bluffing," Simon said, stepping backward through the darkness.

Then his heel touched the concrete of the far wall. They had reached the other side.

Simon pulled out his phone and turned on the flashlight. He shined it into the corner.

Abby wasn't there.

They were alone with the demon in the basement.

And they were in the far corner, far away from the stairs.

"Simon," Virgil said again, this time with more urgency. "We should get out of here."

"Yeah," Simon nodded, sweat suddenly beading up on his forehead. "Let's go." They started walking back toward the stairs.

"One second, if I might," Asag said from across the room, bathed in blood-red light. And even though there was a gulf of open space between them, and even though Virgil had the flame that would protect them from his approach, Asag's voice was so commanding that Virgil stopped dead in his tracks. "You brought a lighter this time instead of a candle, is that right?" he asked. He took a step closer, and Virgil held the flame up higher, as if it might make the protection spell stronger. Asag held up his hands innocently and shuffled to a stop. "Candles are made to burn for hours at a time. Do you know how long a small, cheap, toy lighter will stay lit?"

Virgil looked at Simon. Simon shook his head. "Move," he whispered.

But Virgil couldn't. He was suddenly rooted to the ground with fear. "No," he said in answer to the demon. His voice was small and terrified.

Asag lifted his left arm and made a big show of looking at his watch. "I'd say you probably have until about...now."

As soon as he said it, the flame burned through the last of the lighter's fuel. The purple light sputtered, sparked, and disappeared.

"Oh, no," Simon whispered.

The demon moved like a power surge. He exploded from the far side of the room, moving toward them so fast the air screamed as he tore through it. Virgil screamed too, and he dropped the lighter, throwing up his hands to protect himself. In the darkness, two bright, orange platters spun to life from the palms of his hands, and the demon collided with the shields. Virgil was knocked backward, and he and Simon slammed into the back wall. But Asag fell backward, too, stumbling back from the force of the collision, losing his own footing and falling onto his seat.

For a few moments, no one spoke. Simon and Virgil was surprised to be alive, and the demon was just as stunned to have been rebuffed by the mortal's energy shield. Asag scrambled to his feet and kept a safe distance, regarding them curiously. He paced before them like a tiger in a cage. "You've learned some new tricks," he said, his voice coming out grating and hard, like two stones rubbing together. "Studying with a kinesthetic?" he surmised.

Simon's brain slowly began to unstick itself from the shock of having been rushed by the demon. His thoughts began to tumble more clearly into view. "Virgil," he whispered. "Open your vault."

"My—?" Virgil began, sounding confused. But then it clicked, and he actually grinned. "Right. Got it. Give me a second."

"I'm going to give you a window. Ready?"

Virgil closed his eyes. "Quiet, I'm opening my vault."

"Great." Simon gritted his teeth. He let the anger and sadness and joy of his life well up in his chest. He pictured Abby, and his mom, and the Appalachian woods, and the blank space that was his dad, and the gravestone with Laura's name.

Then he took all those emotions, and he set them free.

He lunged toward Asag with his fists glowing with hot orange light. He screamed a warrior's cry as he let loose with his right hand, then with his left. Two huge energy balls burst forward; the first sailed over Asag's shoulder, but the second caught him in the neck, exploding in a fiery burst, and the demon fell backward, howling in pain. Simon dropped to one knee and clapped both of his hands together. He pushed his magic back down his arms, and with the energies combined, both of his closed fists began to radiate a white-hot light that filled the room. Asag looked up from the floor, holding out his hands to block the strike. Simon let the energy loose, and it exploded out like a comet, leaving a long trail of kinesthetic light. Asag crossed his arms in front of his face, and the blast hit him in his big, meaty forearms. The force of the energy shoved him back, and the demon went sliding across the floor.

"Virgil!" Simon cried. "Now!"

He ducked out of the way, and Virgil stepped forward. He held the glowing wooden ball in his hand. "This is the coolest thing I've ever done," he said as he took three steps, windmilled his arm behind him, and threw the ball at the demon with as much underhand force as he could muster.

The ball rocketed across the room, and it caught Asag square in the face. He screamed in pain as the porcelain mask shattered, its delicate shards tinkling to the concrete floor like pieces of a broken window. The force of the impact spun the demon around. He was huddled on the floor on his knees with his back turned to the two young men.

Simon and Virgil stood uncertainly, not knowing what to do next. The demon breathed heavily with anger, his shoulders shaking as he clutched his injured head. "I don't think you should have gone for the face," Simon whispered, a deep sense of dread spreading through his stomach.

"I didn't. The ball did." The wooden weapon pulled a U-turn around the room and zoomed back into Virgil's open hand.

"Keep that handy," Simon advised. "I don't think this is over."

Asag pushed himself up to his feet. His shoulders heaved with anger. He turned slowly in the pulsing red light, his hands covering his face. He continued to turn until he was standing directly before the two young men. He seemed somehow larger; his head was actually scraping the floor above, and his shoulders were so wide that they took up half of the room, at least. The light reflected off his scales, producing a fiery, shimmering effect that rippled across his skin. The porcelain baby mask lay shattered on the floor.

The demon lowered his hands, revealing his true face.

Virgil screamed.

Simon was so scared, his throat choked out any sound before it could escape.

The demon's face looked like it had been bashed in with a stone. It was concave, with sharp, broken bones protruding through scaly skin. A lightning bolt-shaped splinter of rock had been stabbed through each eye, and the jagged ends of them protruded from his sunken eye holes, dribbling wet, black bloody mucous. The middle of his face had been jammed back through his razor-sharp teeth, which dripped with the same viscous black blood. Each tooth was as long and sharp as a needle. They were fully exposed down beyond the dark, wet gum line, to the bones that connected his jaw to the back of his skull. They could see through the ragged hole in his soft palate on top when he opened his mouth, to the space where off-white maggots squirmed in his caved-in sinus cavities, feeding on the rot of his flesh that had been dying inside for millennia.

"My throat is a gateway to hell," the blind demon rasped, the black mucous bubbling visibly in his mouth as he spoke. "The last thing you see in this world will be my teeth tearing your eyes from your head."

He lunged forward and swiped at Virgil. Simon pushed his friend out of the way, putting himself in the path of Asag's claw. The demon caught him on the shoulder, and his sharp nails sank into Simon's flesh. He screamed and tried to wrench himself free, but before he could, Asag pulled back his arm, and Simon went with it. His shoulder slid off the claws as he arced through the air, and he went flying across the room, slamming hard into the far wall. He shook his head, dazed, and watched dumbly as the demon approached Virgil, who had huddled into the corner. As Asag closed in, Virgil threw the Skee-Ball curio, but the demon was too close, and he smacked it out of Virgil's hand just as it left his grip. Virgil reacted quickly, shooting an energy blast at the demon, but his hand was shaking, and the shot went wide. With the other hand, he formed a kinesthetic shield, and he cowered behind it. The demon screamed, raised his fists over his head, and brought them down hard on the shield, again, and again, and again, until the magic cracked, then splintered, with tiny orange-light chunks sprinkling the basement floor around Virgil's feet.

Simon weakly raised a hand and willed his energy into his arm. His arm glowed dimly, and he pushed the blast out of his hand, but it was such a feeble burst that it dropped halfway across the room and fell to the floor, dissipating against the concrete in a watery pool of light.

This is the end, he thought. He looked across the room at the fear that filled Virgil's eyes as the demon stood over him, relishing his victory. "I'm so sorry, Virgil," he whispered.

He lowered his eyes and waited for it to be over.

Just then, a hole opened up in the ceiling, and two metal rings dropped out of it, clattering to the floor. As soon as it appeared, the circle closed, but as it was shrinking, Simon saw a familiar ice-blue glow peering down at him from above.

He looked at the metal pieces that had fallen through the portal. They weren't just any metal rings; they were manacles. Simon instantly sat up and dove for the gray metal cuff. He snapped it onto his wrist and pushed his will into his hand. He saw the manacle become bright with energy, and he straightened his arm, propping it up with his free hand, aiming it at Asag's back.

He would only get one shot.

Simon held his breath, and he fired.

The concentrated energy bullet fired across the room and ripped through Asag's shoulder, just as his arm was coming down on Virgil's unprotected skull. The bullet tore a hole through the demon's flesh, and the creature bellowed in pain. His arm dropped to his side, missing Virgil's head by a few inches.

Virgil took the chance and crawled away from the demon, ducking under his other arm and scooting toward the center of the room.

"Virgil!" Simon yelled. "Catch!" He picked up the ivory manacle and launched it toward Virgil. Virgil caught it against his chest as Asag turned, his left arm hanging useless from his injured shoulder. He raised his right arm above his head, and it became pliable, changing shape until his hand was a great hammer, and his arm was the handle. Virgil clamped the manacle around his wrist and raised his hand as Asag brought the hammer down toward him. With his other hand, Virgil made a shield and crossed that hand over his manacled arm. The kinesthetic shield absorbed the blow of the hammer, breaking into pieces. Asag reared back and prepared to strike again, but by then, Virgil had collected enough power in his manacle, and he blasted it up at the demon's face at point-blank range. The energy bullet ripped through Asag's chin, splattering black blood across the ceiling. Asag screamed, and Virgil rolled over, hopped to his feet, and sprinted across the basement to the place where Simon stood.

"Let's get out of here," Virgil said, veering toward the stairs.

But Simon grabbed his elbow, stopping him cold. "No," he said. "Let's finish this."

He nodded down at the floor. Virgil didn't see anything at first, the room was so dark, and he pleaded with his eyes for them to leave. But then the red light pulsed brightly, and he saw something lying on the floor.

It was the third item that Llewyn had dropped through the portal in the ceiling: a hammered piece of black iron with a spherical knob handle on one end and an arrow-sharp point on the other. It looked like a stunted fireplace poker.

Simon picked it up and examined it in the dim light.

"What do we do with that?" Virgil asked.

Simon held it up so Virgil could get a good look. "I'm guessing the pointy end goes into the demon," he said.

Virgil sighed. He took a few quick breaths, shook out his neck, and said, "Screw it. Let's send Asag back to hell, or die trying."

"Preferably the first one," Simon muttered.

The demon had gathered himself together on the other side of the room. Black blood seeped from his shoulder and dripped from his chin. His entire body quivered with rage. His needle-teeth frothed with dark saliva as he turned to face the two humans. "I am immortal," he rasped, his voice rippling with the blood that clotted his throat. "My story is eternal. Yours ends tonight, in blood."

Simon tightened his grip on the iron stake and sent energy into his manacle. Virgil's manacle glowed, too, and his right hand reached out and formed a circular shield. They stood shoulder to shoulder, facing the demon with their teeth bared.

"Ready?" Simon asked.

"Ready," Virgil confirmed.

They gave each other a nod.

Then they ran full-speed at the demon.

CHAPTER 25

Asag sprang into action, exploding toward them with incredible speed. He brought his fist screaming toward Virgil. Virgil deflected it with the shield, and Simon blasted Asag with an energy bullet to the stomach. The demon reeled, spinning around and catching Simon with the backside of his hand. Simon went flying across the room, landing in a heap on the floor.

Virgil, who had been knocked over by the impact on his shield, rolled onto his back and shot up at the demon from his wrist. His energy blast ripped through Asag's hip, and he buckled down to one knee, screaming with rage. Virgil held out his left hand, and the wooden ball zoomed into it from across the room. It glowed with light as he smashed it against the side of Asag's head, and the demon went toppling to the ground.

"Simon, we're doing it!" Virgil cried, pushing himself to his feet! "We're actually doing—" But he didn't get to finish. Asag clapped his hands together, then pulled them apart, revealing a brimstone staff that he conjured up from an unseen realm, and used it to bash in Virgil's left shoulder. His bones cracked audibly, and Virgil fell to the ground, howling with pain.

Simon felt himself bubbling up with rage. He struggled to his feet, and he swiped the iron poker through the air a few times. He raised his left arm and gathered energy into his manacle. Then he ran forward, yelling a warrior's cry as the power built there. He fired a shot, aiming for the demon's heart. But Asag was ready, and he side-stepped it easily. The energy bullet ricocheted off the stairwell and shot up to the ceiling, burning a hole into the wood.

Simon, propelled forward by his anger, raised the poker above his head and prepared to drive it into the demon's chest.

But Asag reached out with one massive hand and caught Simon by the throat before he could get within striking distance. He lifted Simon into the air. Simon's feet kicked as they left the ground, and he gagged and choked as Asag's hand crushed his windpipe. He scraped at Asag's fingers with his free hand, but the demon had a strong grip, and Simon was no match for it. Black stars crept into Simon's vision as his body began to go slack from the lack of oxygen.

Virgil staggered to his feet. In a cruel joke of fate, his left arm now mirrored Asag's...broken, and hanging limply at his side. He blinked hard, trying to bring the world into focus, but the pain of his shattered shoulder was sending everything into a tilting haze. Through his blurred vision, he saw the demon lifting Simon with his good hand, lifting him high above the basement floor, almost high enough that Simon's head could brush the ceiling. Simon was kicking his legs frantically, fighting for breath and scrabbling against the demon's hand, but Asag's grip was too strong. He was literally choking the life out of Virgil's best friend.

Virgil lifted his right arm and focused as much energy as he could into his manacle. Asag saw the ivory cuff come to life, and he turned, swinging Simon's helpless body around like a shield between Virgil and the demon. Virgil cried out in helplessness, and he shifted his focus, letting the energy drain away from his cuff. Simon's head lolled back on his shoulders, and his dark, dying eyes rolled over to lock on Virgil. A single tear spilled over Simon's cheek, and in his eyes, Virgil saw his friend's pleading, desperate, lonely goodbye.

But he also saw something else: the iron poker dangling from Simon's hand.

Virgil gritted his teeth. "Not yet," he vowed, locking eyes with Simon and filling himself with stubborn energy. He drew himself up to his full height as Asag opened the mechanism that passed for his mouth. The demon's needle-teeth opened wide, moving closer to Simon's face. Simon saw the steel in Virgil's eye, and saw him nodding at the spike in his hand, and suddenly he understood. Asag lowered his great, gaping mouth toward him, and as the light began to fade in his eyes, Simon focused all his strength on his right arm, and he lifted the iron arrow up, his arm trembling from the effort.

Virgil tried to ignore the blinding pain from his left arm as he brought his right wrist up to his teeth and clacked the ivory manacle against his mouth. After a few clumsy bumps, his teeth found the release button, and the manacle fell away. Thus freed, Virgil's hand began to glow. Virgil reached down deep into the pits of his memory, drawing every bit of joy, every bit of pain, every bit of triumph and loss that he could muster, and he sent it all into his hand. His fist changed color, from orange to yellow to white, as the energy in his body built to an extraordinary level. Virgil pressed all the emotion he had into his palm, and when he had dredged up every memory and every bit of energy he could stand, he opened his hand, and the power burst out into a thick, circular shield, heavier and more powerful than any he had yet created. It spread from his palm like a tangible halo, and this time, it was so strong and precise that the runes of some ancient language glowed in the rim of the kinesthetic armor.

Simon raised his arm as high as his faltering body would allow. The sharp end of the iron arrow pointed directly at Asag's heart. Virgil stepped up, ignoring the ache in his left shoulder, and he leapt into the air, screaming with pain and fury and frustration and courage, bringing his right hand spinning through the air. As he came back down, he swung his shield, and it struck the knob end of Simon's iron poker, slamming into it like a hammer, and the stake drove down, straight into the demon's heart, pushing through the evil, beating flesh of it, bursting through the muscle.

Asag roared in pain and surprise. He loosened his grip on Simon's throat, and Simon went crashing to the floor, gasping for air and holding his neck. Asag stumbled backward, staring down incredulously at the poker sticking out of his chest. Then his body began to contort grotesquely; his chest caved in, and then his torso ratcheted up, and then his legs were sucked in, and Simon and Virgil watched in horror as the demon slowly collapsed.

The hell-portal in his throat was pulling him home.

"*Noooo!*" Asag screeched, flailing his arms, trying to grab ahold of the poker and pull it out of his chest. "*Noooooooo!*" But it was too late. His body pulled in on itself like a dying star, and with a wet, sickening *POP,* the demon was gone.

CHAPTER 26

Simon and Virgil limped up the stairs and up to the door. The demon had taken with him the pulsing light and the feeling of dread that had seemed to fill every corner, and now the basement was just another dark, damp, unremarkable basement. Simon reached the top of the stairwell first, and the door opened easily at his touch.

"How's your arm?" he asked with a frown.

"Hurts," Virgil replied. He placed his wooden ball back into his psychic vault, then he gripped his upper arm and held it close to his body to keep its movements to a minimum. The pressure made him draw a deep, pained breath.

"We have to get you to a hospital," Simon decided.

"Not yet," Virgil winced.

"Why not?"

"Because we still haven't found Abby," Virgil said. "And I think I know where she is."

Simon sighed. He looked up at Mrs. Grunberg's old house. "Yeah…I think I do, too."

Up on the second floor, a figure stood at the window, looking down at them. The figure was backlit by a dim lamp. They couldn't make out the person's features, but neither of them had any doubt that it was Neil Grunberg.

"All right, I'll go in and see what I can see," Simon said. "You go wait in the car. Or, better yet, call an ambulance. I'll meet you at the hospital." He turned to go, but Virgil grabbed him with his good hand.

"No way," Virgil insisted. "We're in it together. 'Til the end."

"Virgil, your arm is totally broken," Simon replied. "It looks like a wet noodle. You need to go to a doctor."

"Well, it's not going to get any *more* broken if I don't go for another hour."

Simon gaped at his friend. "Yes, Virgil. Yes, it will. You'll flop it into something, or you'll forget that it's broken and try to use your hand, you are going to *severely* hurt yourself. And we have no idea what we're up against, here." Simon looked back up at the window and shivered. The silhouette was gone. "I'm starting to think Neil might be less innocent in all this than we thought."

"Yeah. I didn't want to say anything earlier, but I'm pretty sure I saw a second shadow standing next to *his* shadow when we all went upstairs. And that usually only happens when there's actually someone there to *make* the shadow."

"I saw it too," Simon admitted.

"And he keeps calling his grandma's bedroom 'the sleeping room.' And that makes me think it's not a bedroom at all."

"Right."

"Right. So let's find something to use for a sling, and let's go see what Neil the Necromancer is hiding upstairs."

Simon nodded reluctantly. "Okay," he decided. "But stay behind me. And keep your right hand ready to fire."

"Yes, sir," Virgil said. He gave Simon a mock salute. "Ow."

"Good. This is going well." Simon rolled his eyes. "Come on. We'll use a dish towel from the kitchen to wrap you up." He crossed over to the kitchen door and turned the knob. It was locked. "Great. What do we do now, break a window?"

"Hey," Virgil said, looking at the keyhole. "Try your key."

"What key? My magic key?"

Virgil nodded. "Yeah."

"Why would my magic key open Mrs. Grunberg's kitchen door?"

Virgil shrugged his good shoulder. "I mean, I honestly think the better question is, why *wouldn't* your magic key open Mrs.

Grunberg's kitchen door? It's supposed to be helpful when we need it."

Simon exhaled. "Fine." He closed his eyes and pictured his vault. He punched the numbers on the keypad, and the door fell open. In his imagination, he reached into the vault and retrieved the key. When he opened his eyes, he was holding it in his hand. "That is never going to not be weird," he decided.

"It is so, so cool," Virgil agreed.

Simon slipped the key into the door. The lock turned smoothly.

"Huh," Simon said.

"That is a very specifically useful magic key," Virgil added.

They crept into the kitchen. Simon grabbed a dish towel from the counter, and he carefully, if not painlessly, fashioned the towel into a sling for Virgil's broken arm. Virgil closed his eyes and clenched his teeth the entire time, biting back the tears that bubbled up from the pain. But in the end, Simon did a pretty decent job, and Virgil's arm hung more or less comfortably in the cotton sling.

"Hm. Not bad," Virgil offered.

"Maybe I should go to med school," Simon muttered. "Let's go."

They walked quietly through the parlor, both of them on high alert. Virgil stored some kinesthetic energy in his manacle, and Simon was careful to return his magic key to his psychic vault before powering up his manacle as well.

They made it to the bottom of the stairwell. Neil stood on the landing above, his hands gripping the wooden railing. His face was red, and seething with anger. *"What did you do?!"* he screamed. *"What did you do to Asag?!"*

"Neil," Simon said evenly, trying to keep his voice calm as he mounted the first stair, "maybe you should take a few deep breaths."

"Don't you tell me what to do," Neil snarled. His blood flushed hotly through his pale skin, giving his face a red, splotchy appearance.

"Neil, what did the demon do to you?" Virgil asked, climbing the stairs slowly behind Simon.

"Did he make you…like this?" Simon asked, gesturing up at Neil's general appearance. "Is he the reason you can't sleep?"

"He was going to set me free," Neil whispered, his lips quivering with rage. *What did you do to him?*"

"We sent him home," Simon replied. He was halfway up the stairs now. "You can relax, Neil. He's out of the basement now. We sent him back to hell."

Neil howled with rage. It was a startling sound, more animal than human. It stopped Simon on the stairwell, but Virgil kept going, and bumped into him with his broken arm.

"Ow!" Virgil cried.

Simon frowned. "Sorry." He turned his attention back up to Neil, but the boy had disappeared. "Uhh…Virg?"

"What?"

"Where'd the psychopath go?"

They climbed the rest of the stairs. It was dark on the second floor, and they couldn't quite tell how many doors there were leading off from the landing, or how many lined the hallway that led to the bathroom. "Well, this will be a fun game," Virgil said. He nodded toward the first door on their left. "Should we see what's behind Door Number One?"

Simon eased open the door and peeked inside. It was a closet, full of mundane cleaning supplies. "Nope."

"Door Number Two, then," Virgil said. They crept along to the next door. It, too, was unlocked, and Simon pulled open the door.

"Holy…" His voice trailed off as he gazed around the room.

"Okay," Virgil said, looking in over Simon's shoulder. "This must be Neil's room."

There was no bed inside, just a few blankets piled into a mound in the corner. The wooden floorboards had been painted black, and there was a huge pentagram drawn on the floor in white chalk. A podium stood in the center of the five-pointed star, with two thick, black candles flanking an old, dusty, leather-bound book. The flames from the candles threw long, quivering shadows across the floor and softly illuminated what appeared to be splotches of dried blood. There were some clothes scattered around the room, a few candy wrappers, and half a dozen empty Starbucks cups. But it was otherwise empty. Neil wasn't inside.

"I think maybe Neil should talk to a therapist," Virgil decided.

And then, even though there was no one else inside the room, the door knob turned, as if someone was twisting it on the other side. Then the open door began to push itself closed, with enough pressure behind it that Simon was nudged out of the doorway as it shut. Through the flickering candlelight coming through the slit beneath the door, they could see the shadows of two legs stretching across the floor.

"There's someone on the other side," Virgil whispered, his eyes wide with horror.

"No," Simon replied, suddenly as white as a sheet. "There's not."

Virgil reached up and turned the knob, just to test it.

It was locked.

"I don't like this, I don't like this, I don't like this," he murmured in short, scared bursts.

Then there was the sound of a muffled woman's scream from a room further down the hall.

Simon broke into a run, and Virgil hurried along behind him, babying his injured arm. They reached the room where the woman was screaming. Simon tried the knob, but of course, it was locked. He pressed his ear to the door. "Abby?" he called out. The screaming got louder.

"Stand back," Simon said to Virgil, and loud enough for someone else on the other side of the door to hear. He took a step backward, then raised his leg and kicked at the door as hard as he could.

Simon's foot slammed against the wood, which barely budged. A shockwave of pain shot through his knee, and he hobbled down the hall, cursing under his breath and hissing away the pain.

"Who are you, Steven Segal? You can't break down a door!" Virgil chided him. "Use your key!"

"The key's not going to open every single lock!" Simon shot back.

"It's worth a try!"

Simon retrieved the key from his psychic vault and jammed it into the door's lock. He turned it, and the door fell open.

Simon took a second to marvel at the magic key. "I take back all the bad things I said about you," he whispered, giving the key a quick kiss before returning it to the vault. Then he sprang through the door, throwing up a shield with his right hand just in time to catch a blast of dark purple magic that shot at him from across the door. The force of the impact knocked him back, and he hit the corner of the door before tumbling to his knees.

Virgil dove in behind Simon, and he fired a shot blindly into the corner of the room where the blast had come from.

"Virgil! Don't!" Simon cried.

Virgil's shot sailed above Neil's head and exploded through the wood paneled wall. It had missed Abby's hand by only inches.

"Whoops," Virgil said.

The whole tableau came into focus then. They were in a study, an oak-paneled room with bookshelves on two walls filled with old, leather-bound books, most of which were coated thickly with dust, as if they hadn't been touched in decades. There was a massive wooden desk near the far end of the room; Neil was crouched behind it, using it for cover. Abby was shackled to the wall behind the desk, her wrists secured by two thick, iron cuffs that were attached to heavy chains that disappeared into the wall. Her feet were chained, too, and a piece of duct tape had been affixed over her mouth. Her eyes were wide with terror.

"*You're not supposed to be in the standing room!*" Neil screamed. He reached up from behind the desk, and they could see that he was holding some sort of stick in his hand. He aimed it at Simon, and another bolt of purple lightning shot out of the end. Simon dove out of the way, and the lightning tore through the bookshelf behind him, burning a hole in one of the books.

"Neil! Stop!" Simon urged, throwing up his hands to show that they were empty of any weapon or magic. "You don't have to do this! Asag is gone!"

"Do you have any idea what I went through to bring that demon into this plane of existence?" he demanded. "What I had to *sacrifice?!*"

Virgil looked over at the redheaded boy, confused. "Wait, you summoned Asag? On *purpose?*"

Neil didn't respond. Instead, he threw a magic blast blindly back toward Virgil, and it missed him by almost a whole foot.

"I was going to sacrifice your friend to appease Asag, and to make him strong enough be unleashed on Templar," Neil snarled from behind the desk. "He was the next step in the Great Plan, and you've ruined everything! So now I'm going to kill her as punishment!"

"Neil! Listen to me," Simon pleaded, taking a step closer to the desk, his hands still held up. "You're sick. But we can help you get better. Okay? Let Abby go, and put down the wand, and let's leave here together."

"I have to go to the hospital anyway...we can drop you at the psych ward," Virgil suggested. Simon shot him a sharp look. Virgil tilted his head and mouthed, *What?*

"I'm not sick. I'm *chosen*," Neil said. "He chose *me!* Out of all of them!"

Simon furrowed his brow. "Who chose you? Asag?"

Neil snorted. "No, not *Asag*. Asag was a tool. A puppet! But I was *chosen,* and now you've *ruined it!*" He leapt to his feet and fired three shots at Simon. Simon threw up shields with both hands, barely spreading them out in time. The shields absorbed the magic, pushing Simon back half a step.

Abby pleaded at Simon with her eyes. Tears rolled down her cheeks. Simon's heart broke seeing her that way. He couldn't imagine what she must have been feeling.

Feeling...

"That's it," he whispered.

Neil whirled around, pressing the wand to Abby's throat. She flinched at the touch of it, and she squeezed her eyes shut. "Now you get to watch her die!" Neil shrieked.

"Virgil," Simon instructed, "ball." Virgil nodded and closed his eyes, reaching into his psychic vault. Simon shifted his attention to Abby. He called out her name, and she opened her eyes. "Abby," he said again, connecting with her eyes. "Pre-frontal cortex."

Abby's eyes grew large with understanding. She nodded, almost imperceptibly.

The tip of Neil's wand began to glow purple. "You'll watch, and you'll always know that *you* were the one who was responsible for her death!" Neil screamed. "You, and your meddling, and your pathetic excuse for magic! I was the chosen one! *I* was *chosen!*"

"Virgil!" Simon shouted. "Now!"

Virgil gripped the Skee-Ball ball and rolled it on the floor. It spun forward, picking up speed as it rolled beneath the desk and rocketed upward, slamming into Neil's shin. Neil screamed and doubled over in pain, hitting the floor and bringing the wand with him. Simon powered up his manacle and aimed it carefully at Abby's wrist. He fired a beam of magic; it found its mark and melted through the chain links. Abby reached her newly-freed hand up to her lips, pulled off the duct tape, and tore off her glove with her teeth. Then she reached down with her bare hand just as Neil was rearing back up, preparing to fire his wand at Virgil. When he stood up, Abby touched his cheek, and she absorbed his feelings...and she sent them back into him, magnified, and then pulled them out again, and then sent them back again, magnified even more, back and forth in a closed loop of emotion that overloaded Neil's prefrontal cortex. His eyes rolled up into his head, and he moaned as he fell over onto the floor, unconscious.

Virgil stood up. He let the wooden ball roll back into his hand. He glanced suspiciously down at Neil's prostrate body and said, "So...what just happened, exactly?"

Abby pressed her lips together a few times, working out the pain of having torn off the tape, then she gave Simon a grin. "Correct me if I'm wrong," she said, "but I think we just became heroes of Templar."

Simon exhaled, and he allowed himself a smile. "Yeah," he said. "I think we just did."

CHAPTER 27

"So the standing room was a room where he chained people to the wall so they were forced to stand?" Llewyn asked.

They were sitting around a campfire in Llewyn's forest room, the smoke from the flames curling up toward the ceiling and disappearing through a hole he'd opened in the roof with a wave of his hand. The ceiling was now black to match the night sky outside, and dotted with stars that twinkled like the real thing.

Virgil held his hands out over the fire and nodded. "Yep."

The wizard frowned. He rubbed his chin. "Then do I want to know what the sleeping room was?"

"Actually, the sleeping room turned out to just be a bedroom," Simon replied. "We found Mrs. Grunberg sleeping soundly. It looks like maybe Neil had her under a sleeping spell. She doesn't remember a thing."

"Hey, thanks for sending the manacles, by the way," Virgil said. "And that iron arrow or whatever."

"The Brimstone Spire," Llewyn said, nodding. "A powerful weapon against black hearts."

"We appreciate you using some of your magic to send it to us," Simon said, almost guiltily.

But Llewyn waved him off. "It was what needed doing," he said. Then he added, "You're welcome."

Abby frowned at the fire, lost in her memory of the evening. "She sure looked confused when the police took her grandson away," she said.

"Who? Mrs. Grunberg?" Virgil asked. "Yeah. She did. But to be fair, so did the police. You'd think they'd never arrested a practitioner of the dark arts before or something."

Llewyn snorted. "They had better get used to it. When the boy summoned Asag, he opened a door. Asag blocked that door, while he was in this realm. Now that he's gone, the door is wide open."

Simon looked up, alarmed. "Are you telling me we just left a door to hell wide open in Mrs. Grunberg's basement?"

But Llewyn shook his head. "Not in the basement. And not a door to hell, exactly. But the impermeable wall between our reality and another, darker dimension has been breached. Asag was just the beginning. The first big incident. Demon Zero." He pulled out his flask and drank deeply. He wiped his mouth on his sleeve, and added, "Many more will come." He furrowed his brow, looking troubled. "Many, many more."

"More demons?" Abby asked.

"Not *just* demons. More dark creatures of all sorts." He looked up at the three of them, his blue eye blazing behind its patch. "You did good work casting Asag out. But make no mistake; our war against the darkness is just beginning."

Simon squired a little in his seat. "Llewyn...we saw something strange inside the house, with Neil. It was...a shadow, I guess. The shadow of a man, but there was no man there. It was standing next to Neil's shadow. And then at one point...it slammed a door on us."

"It didn't want us in Neil's magic room," Virgil said, nodding his agreement. "And it was strong. Strong enough to push us out when it closed the door."

"I saw it too," Abby confirmed. "More than once. It was almost always by his side. Or at least, by his shadow's side."

"And Neil kept saying he'd been 'chosen,'" Virgil reminded them. "But not by Asag."

Llewyn made a quiet grunting sound and took another drink from his flask as he considered this new piece of information. "Perhaps the first general in the evil's army has already arrived," he said cryptically. And he didn't elaborate on what he meant when they pressed him.

Virgil took a deep breath, then exhaled slowly, blowing the air out loudly through his lips. "Well. Guess it's a good thing I've got Gladys, then." He tossed the Skee-Ball ball a few times into the air.

"Gladys?" Abby said, raising an eyebrow.

"That's what I named her," Virgil said proudly. "Doesn't she look like a Gladys?"

Simon glanced up at the silhouettes of the trees against the starry sky. The air was still, the fire was warm, and the sounds of crickets and owls willowed in the background. All in all, looking back at the last six years since Laura's death, Simon couldn't remember ever feeling so at peace.

Except for the whole "imminent evil rising" thing.

"So what do we do now?" he asked, watching the sparks from the fire pop in the crisp evening air.

"Personally, I'd like to get back to Skee-Ball," Virgil said. He shook his head ruefully. "That Nerf gun…it mocks me."

The rest of the group ignored him. "Your training will continue, if the experience with Asag and the boy hasn't put you off," Llewyn said.

Simon glanced over at Virgil. "I'm in if you are," he said.

Virgil grinned. "I've actually been thinking about that," he replied, suddenly jumping up to his feet. He began to pace excitedly around the fire. "You don't have a job, and now that Papa Wizard over here keeps me in cash, I don't need a real job, either." Llewyn bristled at the new nickname, but Virgil pressed on: "Given that we're the heroes of Templar now, and that our wizard powers are only going to get bigger and cooler, I think we should hang our own shingle."

"What does that mean?" Simon asked warily.

"You know, start our own place! Our own...I don't know... evil-fighting firm, or whatever! We'll be like private investigators, but with magic powers, and who cast evil demons back to hell! I even have a name for us." He held up his hands and moved them through the air, as if picturing the name in lights. "Dark Matter Investigations."

"Huh. Simon Dark and Virgil Matter." Abby adjusted her glasses on her nose. "It actually seems too convenient to *not* use it."

"Hm. I like it," Llewyn decided.

"And he's our big investor, so now we have to do it," Virgil teased. He sat back down, perched on the edge of his seat, and looked earnestly at Simon. "What do you think?" he asked.

Simon considered the question. They had cast away a serious evil when they defeated Asag, there was no question about that. There was no telling how many lives the demon might have claimed. Or that Neil would have claimed, for that matter, if he had been allowed to keep at his dark work. Even if they had saved one life, it had been worth it.

He thought about all the lives they could save if they truly dedicated themselves to the craft of magic, and to protecting the people of Templar. He wondered how many Lauras there were in the city, how many innocent people who wouldn't have to die or disappear because he and Virgil had taken up the watch. "What do I think," he repeated, looking into the warmth of the flames. He sighed. "I'll tell you what I think."

Virgil tented his hands in front of his mouth and peered out nervously between his fingers. "Yeah?" he asked, practically bouncing with anticipation.

Simon let a wide grin spread across his face.

"I think Dark Matter Investigations is officially open for business."

SIMON AND VIRGIL WILL RETURN IN:

SCORCHED EARTH

BOOK TWO OF
THE DARK MATTER SERIES

ABOUT THE AUTHOR

Clayton Smith is an award-winning Midwestern writer who once erroneously referred to himself as a "national treasure." He is the author of several novels, short story collections, and plays, including the best-selling Apocalypticon series. His short fiction has been featured in national literary journals, including Canyon Voices and Write City Magazine.

He is also rather tall.

Find him online StateOfClayton.com and on social media as @Claytonsaurus.